BUZZING

BUZZING

Written by Samuel Sattin

Illustrated by Rye Hickman

Little, Brown and Company

New York Boston

About This Book

This book was edited by Aria Balraj and designed by Carolyn Bull. The production was supervised by Kimberly Stella, and the production editor was Lindsay Walter-Greaney. The text was set in ActionFigure BB, and the display type is SuperStrong BB.

Little, Brown Ink
Hachette Book Group
1290 Avenue of the Americas, New York, NY 10104
Visit us at LBYR.com

First Edition: July 2023

Little, Brown Ink is an imprint of Little, Brown and Company.
The Little, Brown Ink name and logo are trademarks of Hachette Book Group, Inc.

Library of Congress Cataloging-in-Publication Data
Names: Sattin, Samuel, author. | Hickman, Rye, illustrator.
Title: Buzzing / written by Samuel Sattin; illustrated by Rye Hickman.

Description: First edition. | New York : Little, Brown and Company, 2023. | Summary: "Isaac is a shy boy with OCD, but one day at school he meets new friends who introduce him to role-playing games, which lead him on a journey of self-discovery and growth"—Provided by publisher.
Identifiers: LCCN 2022029735 | ISBN 9780316628433 (hardcover) | ISBN 9780316628419 (trade paperback) | ISBN 9780316628426 (ebook)
Subjects: CYAC: Graphic novels. | Obsessive-compulsive disorder—Fiction. Fantasy games—Fiction. | Friendship—Fiction. | LCGFT: Graphic novels.
Classification: LCC PZ7.7.S187 So 2023 | DDC 741.5/973—dc23/eng/20220725
LC record available at https://lccn.loc.gov/2022029735

ISBNs: 978-0-316-62843-3 (hardcover), 978-0-316-62841-9 (pbk.), 978-0-316-62842-6 (ebook), 978-0-3163-4555-2 (ebook), 978-0-316-34566-8 (ebook)

PRINTED IN CHINA

APS

Hardcover: 10 9 8 7 6 5 4 3 2 1

Paperback: 10 9 8 7 6 5 4 3 2 1

For the weird kids

Bzzz...

Bzzz...
Isaac.

Bzzzz...
Isaac...
Bzzz...

Remember how stupid you looked this morning?
In the mirror.

Your lips looked uneven.
They *are* uneven. Crooked.

READ FOR FUN!
HOMEWORK:
DON'T ERASE!
Four legs truth,
two legs lie.
PARTS of SPEECH
PRONOUN:
NOUN:
PROPER NOUN
VERB:
ADVERB:
PREPOSITION:
CONTRACTION:
3 types of Writing
You don't deserve friends.
It's better if they don't look at you.
That dragon's wings aren't even.
Crooked like your lips.

"Four legs truth, two legs lie"--pay attention.
Stop smiling.
Stop frowning.
You can't pay attention, can you?
ISAAC?
You don't know the answer.
You can't pay attention, can you?
You don't deserve to know the answer.
two legs lie.
BZZZZZ
ISAAC?
...YES?
WHAT DO YOU THINK SNOWTUFT WAS TRYING TO GET ACROSS IN THIS PHRASE?
I...
He knows you can't pay attention.
Your lips are uneven.

I...
You've got germs. He's got germs.
I...

TO MAKE EVERYONE... LISTEN TO BONAPARTE. BECAUSE HE WANTS... CONTROL.
YES, THAT'S RIGHT.
WHAT BONAPARTE IS MAKING IS CALLED PROPAGANDA. DO ANY OF YOU KNOW WHAT THAT IS?

IT'S WHEN GOVERNMENTS MAKE UP THINGS TO KEEP PEOPLE...

One right answer. So what?
STOP. GO AWAY.
If we stop, Mom will get sick.
It'll be your fault.
Someone will hurt her.

Uneven lips.
Go to the bathroom and look. Maybe you're dying.

HEY!

YOUR NAME'S ISAAC, RIGHT?
Dying...
UH... YEAH.

WELL, I'M MICAH. AND THIS IS JAIME--
MICAH SAID THEY SAW YOU DRAWING A DOPE DRAGON IN YOUR NOTEBOOK.
CAN I SEE?

OH, UH, YOU WANT... Y-YEAH...HERE IT, UH...IS...
You've got germs. Dangerous germs.
They're looking at your uneven lips.

WHOA... CHECK THIS OUT, JAIME.
SO GOOD.
SKETCH!
LEMME SEE, LEMME SEE...
WHOA! YOU'RE RIGHT!
AHEM.

HM. THIS IS QUITE A DISPLAY OF DRAFTING SKILL.
BRAVO, ISAAC. IT IS ISAAC ITKIN, CORRECT?
YES...
Horrible name.

YOUR SKILL IN DRAWING FANTASY SERPENTS SURPASSES OTHERS IN THIS ACADEMY, LEADING ME TO BELIEVE YOU MAY BE A PRIME CANDIDATE FOR OUR NEW TABLETOP ESCAPADE.
WH-WHAT?
MICAH, CAN YOU TRANSLATE?

WHAT CARMEN MEANS IS THAT WE'RE STARTING A SWAMPS & SORCERY GAME.
CORRECT.
SWAMPS & SORCERY?

IT'S AN ADVENTURE GAME, WHERE YOU GET TO PLAY AS DIFFERENT CHARACTERS.
IN A FANTASY WORLD.
ADMINISTERED IN THIS CASE BY ME, AS GM. OR GAME MASTER, IF YOU PREFER.

SO, WHAT DO YOU THINK?

YOU IN?

You've got germs. You're contagious.

It's bad to spread germs.

You shouldn't be around people.

Y-YEAH. THAT SOUNDS LIKE FUN.

...

I'LL SHOW MYSELF OUT.
DID NOAH AND LESLIE SAY YES?
AWESOME.
YEP!

BYE, ISAAC!

UH, BYE!
OH, WAIT. ACTUALLY...

KIND OF HARD TO START OUR ADVENTURE IF I DON'T HAVE YOUR NUMBER.

OH, RIGHT, YEAH, PHONE NUMBERS ARE IMPORTANT. HEH HEH...

Isaac Itkin
(303) 555-4
I'LL BE IN TOUCH.

Remember.
Germs.

Unclean.
Stay away from people. Don't hurt them.

MIRIAM!
UGH. NOT AGAIN.

CAN I ASK YOU A QUESTION?
...WHAT?
YOU KNOW WHAT SWAMPS & SORCERY IS, RIGHT?

YEAH, IT'S A NERD GAME. WHY?
S-SOME KIDS...THEY ASKED ME TO, EHH, PLAY AND...
Because they don't know yet.
How messed up you are.
I MIGHT SUCK. BUT I SAID YES ANYWAY...

IS THAT RIGHT?
ARE YOU GOING TO TELL MOM?
Mom knows you're contaminated.
Loves you anyway. So lucky.
I... UH...

"GAMES LEAD TO COMPULSIONS, DARLING. I THOUGHT WE DISCUSSED YOU WERE TO AVOID THEM."

THAT'S JUST FOR VIDEO GAMES.
You shouldn't have said yes.
REGARDLESS, YOU CAN'T HANDLE IT.

WHO'S THAT?
Dirty.
You'll infect people.
NO ONE.
OHMYGOD, DID YOU HEAR ABOUT WHAT CALVIN DID IN MRS. BAULMUNKE'S CLASS?
I KNOW! SO GROSS.

NO. NO.
THAT'S NOT WHAT I SAID. I CLEARLY REQUESTED THURSDAY.

THEN HAVE *THEM* MOVE THINGS AROUND! I'M NOT THE ONE WHO SCREWED UP.

Too many peas.
YEAH.
YEAH, OK.
Keep the chicken clean.

CLANG

NO WAY...
ISAAC, DARLING...
I MADE THE TEAM!
I THOUGHT WE TALKED ABOUT SECTIONING OFF YOUR FOOD.
OH...YEAH. SORRY.
Weird. Strange.
YOU DON'T HAVE TO SAY SORRY. WE TALKED ABOUT THAT, TOO.
...THE VOLLEYBALL TEAM...
Bad luck.
HOW WAS SCHOOL?
WELL--
B-DING
MIRIAM, PHONES DOWN AT THE DINNER TABLE.
SO. SCHOOL?
NORMAL.
NORMAL HOW?
JUST... NORMAL.
Normal? You?

WHAT, ISAAC? NOT GOING TO TALK ABOUT YOUR NEW GAME GROUP?

GAME GROUP?
UH. WELL.
NOT A VIDEO GAME, THOUGH.
Same thing. You're lying.
WHAT'S IT CALLED, AGAIN? SWORDS & SERPENTS?
SWAMPS & SORCERY.

...WHAT KIND OF A GAME IS IT?
IT'S SOMETHING YOU PLAY WITH FRIENDS--WITH DICE AND MAPS AND STUFF.
Your mom's lips aren't crooked. Why are yours?

DICE AND MAPS?
YEAH.
AND THESE FRIENDS? YOU MET THEM AT SCHOOL?
You don't have friends. They're lying to you.

IN CLASS.
Contaminated.
WHAT ARE THEIR NAMES?
IT'S A FANTASY THING, ISN'T IT? LIKE ELVES AND TROLLS AND STUFF?
UH, YEAH, I THINK SO.

...
WELL, IT'S GOOD THAT YOU'RE MAKING FRIENDS.

THAT REMINDS ME, DARLING. I MADE ANOTHER APPOINTMENT FOR YOU.
WITH DR. PENNY?

Oh no.
MR. BODUM?
WELL, YOU DO HAVE YOUR NORMAL APPOINTMENT WITH DR. PENNY, YES, BUT I MADE ANOTHER ONE WITH YOUR SCHOOL COUNSELOR, MR. BODUM.

BE MINDFUL OF YOUR EAR TUGGING.
YES, MOM.
I'M DONE.
WASH YOUR DISH!
YEAH.

GAMES CAN BE THE WRONG KIND OF ESCAPE FOR PEOPLE WITH YOUR KIND OF OBSESSIVE-COMPULSIVE DISORDER. THEY CAN INTENSIFY COMPULSIONS OR BECOME COMPULSIVE IN THEIR OWN RIGHT.

"IT'S BEST TO LIMIT YOUR EXPOSURE."
...HE WAS TALKING ABOUT VIDEO GAMES.

A GAME IS A GAME.

I'M NOT SAYING YOU CAN'T GET TOGETHER WITH YOUR NEW FRIENDS. I JUST...WANT US TO BE CAREFUL. OK?
OK, MOM.
GRAGAGA

GOOD. NOW GO GET SOME HOMEWORK DONE BEFORE IT'S TIME FOR BED.
AND, ISAAC?

I LOVE YOU.

You didn't get the other side as much.

Too much on this side. Go back.

Hm. Maybe it's because your lips are crooked. Mouth uneven. Deformed?
Spit.

You need to do it again. Or else you'll get sick. What will your mom do?
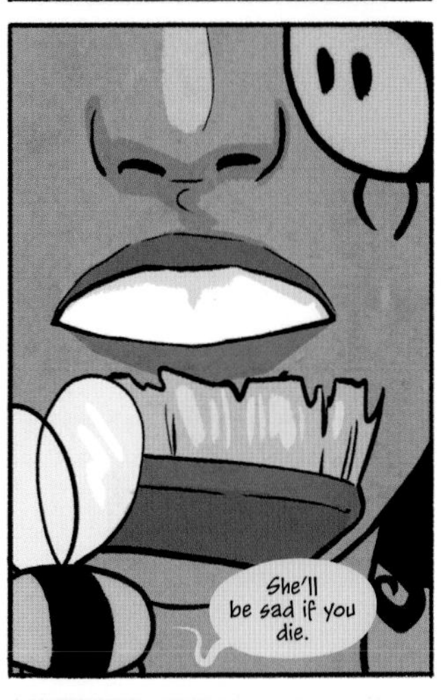
She'll be sad if you die.

One more time.

Better.
Wait! Is your chin crooked, too?
Mutant.

DON'T GET ME STARTED. IT'S, LIKE... SOMETIMES I THINK HE'S FAKING IT.
OHMYGOD, YEAH. YOU READ MY MIND.

She's talking about you.
She's right. It's not real.
You're just a bad person.
CLICK

WHOA... CHECK THIS OUT, JAIME.
Sick.
SO GOOD.
LEMME SEE, LEMME SEE...
WHOA! YOU'RE RIGHT!
SKETCH!
Lies.

KNOCK KNOCK

Lips...chin...
Lips...bzz...
Bzz...

CAN'T YOU DROP ME OFF FIRST?
They're going to hate you.
Remember that or the car will crash.
Your family
R.I.P.
and it'll be your fault.

YOUR LESSON DOESN'T START UNTIL 11.
BUT IT'S ON THE WAY. ISAAC'S FRIENDS ARE ALL THE WAY ACROSS TOWN. YOU'LL HAVE TO GO BACK AND FORTH.
I DON'T MIND.

My stupid brother somehow manages to find kids as geeky as him and they live in the freaking BOONIES

Germs.

SO THAT'S THE GROUP, HUH?
UH...

THAT'S JAIME, AND CARMEN. AND...
Bzzz...
...I THINK THAT'S NOAH AND LESLIE.

GOOD VIBES
MY OTHER RIDE IS A UNICORN
LOVE IS LOVE

ISAAC! SO GLAD YOU'RE HERE.
SO GLAD *I'M* HERE-- HEH!

IS CARMEN READY TO PLAY?
YOU HAVE NO IDEA.
HI! ALICE. SHE/HER.
OH. CLAUDIA. PLEASED TO MEET YOU.

SO. HAVE YOU HEARD ANYTHING ABOUT THIS GAME THEY'RE PLAYING?
HUH? OH, IS THAT WHAT THEY'RE DOING?
I JUST GAVE THE KID A LIFT. THIS ONE PRACTICALLY TAKES CARE OF THEMSELF.

ISAAC! BYE, DARLING!
NICE TO MEET YOU!

ISAAC! WHAT'S UP, MY DUDE?

THIS IS NOAH.
HEY.
AND THIS IS LESLIE.
MORNING!
H-HI! WHAT'S UP?
TRAVELERS!

WELCOME. THE PATH THAT BROUGHT YOU HERE MUST HAVE BEEN ARDUOUS. I'M DELIGHTED TO SEE YOU'RE STILL AMONG THE LIVING.
UH, CARMEN? I DON'T THINK WE'RE PLAYING YET!

SILENCE!
THE MOMENT YOU CROSSED OVER INTO MY DOMINION YOU LEFT YOUR PALTRY FORMER LIVES BEHIND...
AND ENTERED THE STRANGE AND TREACHEROUS WORLD OF--
ADVENTURERS, WELCOME! I'M MAX!

UGH, ***DAAAAD...*** YOU'VE INTERRUPTED MY ENIGMATIC PROLOGUE!
SORRY, CARE-BEAR.
I USED TO PLAY A LITTLE SWAMPS & SORCERY IN MY DAY. AND IF I REMEMBER ANYTHING, A PROPER CAMPAIGN IS NOTHING WITHOUT PROPER ***SNACKS.***

WHOA.

OVER HERE!

...

WELCOME, ADVENTURERS, WAYFARERS, SEEKERS OF ARCANE KNOWLEDGE.
FROM THIS MOMENT FORTH, YOU WILL STOP THINKING OF YOURSELVES AS AWKWARD MIDDLE SCHOOL STUDENTS FROM THE ELEVATED PLAINS OF DENVER--
HEY, I'M NOT AWKWARD--
AND INSTEAD ENVISION A NEW LIFE...

...AS DENIZENS OF RIZULEA.
DENIZENS?

BUT BEFORE WE BEGIN, IT IS YOUR TASK TO CHOOSE THE AVATAR YOU WISH TO REPRESENT YOU ON YOUR QUEST.
HUH?
SHE WANTS US TO CREATE CHARACTERS.
AH.

THIS SHOULD ONLY TAKE FIVE MINUTES.

OK!
YOU'VE FINISHED? GOOD.

NO. BUT I *THINK* I JUST CHOSE MY CLASS.
WHAT?
WHOA. YOU'VE GOTTEN THAT FAR?
I THINK I'M GOING TO BE AN ORC...

GUYS! WE'VE GOT A GAME TO PLAY!
HMM...THE PLAYER'S GUIDE SAYS MAKING A CHARACTER CAN TAKE HOURS.
CARMEN?
CURSE THE SANDS OF TIME...

ALL RIGHT...
MY CHARACTER IS A HUMAN PALADIN, NAMED SER BRIDGER LIGHTBORN!
THEY GO BY THEY/THEM PRONOUNS, CARRY A TWO-HANDED AX PASSED DOWN FROM THEIR GRANDFATHER, AND ARE A SERVANT TO CRUCAS, THE PEACELORD OF THORNGLAMOUR!
I AM AN ORC BARD NAMED BOBBERT THE BRITTLE!
BOBBERT?
HE CARRIES AN ELECTRIC LUTE THAT CHARGES WITH LIGHTNING STRIKES, IS A MASTER AT THROWING DAGGERS, AND IS LOOKING FOR A HERO TO WRITE EPIC METAL BALLADS ABOUT! HE/HIM.
YOU CAN WRITE THEM ABOUT ME!
YEAH!
ROCK ON!

I AM GRUNTUS! FIGHTER. HE/HIM. NO LAST NAME NEEDED.
MOMMY
I'M A HALF-OGRE ORPHAN, SPEAK MOSTLY IN GRUNTS, AND AM COVERED IN HEART TATTOOS.
MY CLUB HAS *MOMMY* CARVED INTO IT.

SHADOW SHADENOIR IS MY NAME. I AM A THIEF. AND THAT'S ALL YOU NEED TO KNOW.
SHE/HER.

GRUNTUS! SHADOW SHADENOIR, PLEASED TO MEET YOU.
GRUNT.
GREETINGS.
♫ *GRUNNNNTUS WITH THE HEART* ♪ ***TATTOOOOOOS!***
♪ *WITHOUT HIS DEAR MOMMY, HE GETS THE* ***BLUUUUUEEEES!*** ♫

What's wrong with you?
So much.
ISAAC! WHAT ABOUT YOUR CHARACTER?
They see how sick you are.

I...UH... I DON'T KNOW...
Better than you.
I DON'T KNOW WHO TO PICK.
They're good. You're bad. You'll screw this up.

THIS WHOLE CHARACTER-MAKING THING *IS* WEIRD.
You're slow.
Slow. Slow. Slow.
Crooked, too.
OK, SO, DO YOU WANT TO PLAY SOMEONE WHO'S KINDA GOOFY OR SMART?

SMART IS GOOD.
You're not smart.
GREAT. AND HOW ABOUT BACKGROUND? DWARF? ELF?
HALF OGRE?
WE ARE *NOT* HAVING TWO HALF OGRES IN THE PARTY.
PLAYER'S

ELF, I GUESS.
Micah's so creative.
You're fake. Admit it. Consequences if not.
AN ELF. COOL.
SO WE HAVE A SMART ELF. IS YOUR CHARACTER STRONG? FAST?
ELF

HE'S STRONG, YEAH...BUT STRONG-MINDED.
BZZ
OH, YOU SHOULD GO FOR A MAGE, THEN.
UH--YEAH! SOUNDS COOL.

OK, I THINK I'VE GOT IT.

M-MY NAME IS VOLIN ARCHIVAST. HE/HIM.
BZZ
Stupid.
I'M A MAGE WHO WAS RAISED TO BE A LIBRARIAN AT THE HALL OF...UH, THE HALL OF MURMURS. AND IT'S MY FIRST TIME...
LEAVING HOME.

BOBBERT THE BARD, AT YOUR SERVICE.
GRUNTUS. GRUNT.
GREETINGS. I'M SHADOW SHADENOIR.

SER BRIDGER LIGHTBORN.
I AM GLAD OUR FATES HAVE CROSSED.

CARMEN! WE'RE READY!
UNGH... HOW MANY DAYS HAS IT BEEN?

WHOA. GUYS. IT'S ALMOST 5!
HOW IS IT SO LATE?!
MICAH, YOU'RE STILL STAYING FOR DINNER, RIGHT?
YEP!

MY MOM'S GOING TO BE HERE IN LESS THAN A MINUTE.
A FULL DAY WASTED. CAST ASIDE LIKE A CHILD'S PLUSHIE AFTER THE COLD, CRUEL ARRIVAL OF ADOLESCENCE.

IT WASN'T WASTED AT ALL!
WE HAVE OUR CHARACTERS DONE NOW, SO WE CAN PLAY FIRST THING NEXT WEEKEND.
EVERYONE'S STILL IN TO KEEP GOING, RIGHT?
YEAH!
HMPH. OK, THEN.

ISAAC! YOUR MOM'S HERE!
WHOA. WHEN YOU SAID SHE'D BE HERE IN LESS THAN A MINUTE, YOU MEANT IT.
HEH, YEAH... MY MOM IS KIND OF SCARY WHEN IT COMES TO BEING PUNCTUAL.

LATER, GUYS! I'LL, UH...
SEE YOU IN SCHOOL!

HI, DARLING.
SEATBELTS ON.
They hate you.

YOU'RE A COUPLE MINUTES LATE. WE'RE SUPPOSED TO PICK UP MIRIAM IN FIFTEEN MINUTES.
AN INTERESTING EXPERIMENT, DRIVING YOU BOTH AROUND ON A SATURDAY.
Car again. Focus on the road lines. Don't make it

FOR
UN!
FINAL EXAM
TOMORROW
NOUN:
PROPER NOUN
VERB:
ADVERB:
PREPOSITION:
CONTRACTION:

...SO REMEMBER THAT TOMORROW'S THE FINAL EXAM.

YOU MIGHT WANT TO HOLD STUDY GROUPS TONIGHT, BUT DON'T GO TOO LATE.

BRRINGGG

OK! SEE YOU ALL TOMORROW!

SO. FREAKING. *AWESOME.*
YOU PROBABLY KNOW THAT ALREADY, RIGHT?
UH...
BZZZ

NO.
IS IT GOOD?
IS IT GOOD?!

IT'S ONLY THE BEST SERIES OF ALL TIME! RIGHT, MICAH?
YUP!

THE CHARACTERS ARE SO COOL.
AND THERE'S THIS WITCH VILLAIN THAT'S SERIOUSLY SCARY.
YEAH. K. J. PROWLER.
"WHY CAN'T WIZARDRY BE LIKE IT USED TO BE?"
I WONDER WHAT SHE'LL DO TO MATIAS.

AND WHAT ABOUT THAT RELATIONSHIP BETWEEN BERTOLD AND JERRY?
I *KNOW.* THEY'RE TOTALLY GOING TO GET TOGETHER.
OR *ARE* THEY?
I NEED BOOK THREE. I JUST *NEED* IT.

YOU HAVEN'T READ THE ELI BOOKS, ISAAC?
UH, NO. BUT...
HERE, BORROW MY COPY.

REALLY?
HECK YES!
THE AUTHOR'S COMING TO THE TATTERED COVER IN A COUPLE OF WEEKS TO RELEASE BOOK THREE.
YOU SHOULD TOTALLY CATCH UP, AND WE CAN ALL GO TOGETHER!

THAT...SOUNDS GREAT.
Going to fail your test.
Micah's smarter than you. Jaime, too.
You don't deserve them.

UGH. JUST HAVE TO FINISH STUDYING FOR THIS FREAKING TEST FIRST.
I'VE GOT TWO TOMORROW.
UNCOOL.
SO UNCOOL.

LATER, ISAAC!
YEAH! LATER!
BEST BOOK EVER.
Bzz... pull your ear...

Do it five times.
Then we'll go.
If you don't pull, you'll fail tomorrow's test.

That's why they don't like you.
Not smart. Not good.
Pull your ear five more times--
HEY-- WATCH OUT!
OOF!

Always in the way.
UGH.
Don't stop pulling or you'll fail your test.
S-SORRY.
Two more times.

WHY IS HE ALWAYS DOING THAT TO HIS EAR?
DOING WHAT?
LIKE... TUGGING IT.

IT JUST...IT MAKES HIM LOOK SO WEIRD, YOU KNOW?
...

GYM IS IN FIVE. WE BETTER GO.
RIGHT!

So weird.

THAT'S WONDERFUL, MIRIAM! SO, THEN, YOU'LL HAVE PRACTICE THREE TIMES PER WEEK?
YEP! TWICE DURING THE SCHOOL WEEK AND ONCE ON SUNDAY.
BUT I CAN CATCH A RIDE WITH HEIDI ON THE WEEKEND, SO YOU DON'T HAVE TO DRIVE ME.

HOW EXCITING. YOU'RE SO ACTIVE AT SCHOOL. IT'S WONDERFUL TO SEE.
THANKS, MOM.

AND DON'T WORRY. I'LL MAKE SURE NOT TO SLACK ON PIANO.
YES, THAT'S IMPORTANT...

OHMYGOD. THAT REMINDS ME. IT WAS SO FUNNY, MOM. IN MY DEBATE CLASS, THERE'S THIS STUDENT NAMED JESS FLOCKNER, AND--
ONE SECOND, MIRIAM.

Uneven.

So weird.

Sick.

Failure.

Your fault.

ISAAC, DARLING?
ARE YOU DOING
OK?
NO!
Sick.

Y...YEAH,
I'M OK.
CAN I
COME IN?

I THOUGHT
YOU'D BE
STUDYING.
HOW LONG
HAVE YOU BEEN
IN HERE?

I DON'T
KNOW...A
LITTLE BIT.

REMEMBER WHAT DR. PENNY SAID ABOUT SPENDING TOO MUCH TIME IN FRONT OF MIRRORS.
YEAH...I REMEMBER.

PREOCCUPYING YOURSELF WITH BODY SYMMETRY GIVES FUEL TO YOUR OBSESSIONS.
REMEMBER, IT'S NEVER JUST "ONE MORE CHECK." YOU CAN'T BARGAIN WITH OBSESSIVE THOUGHTS. BECAUSE--

"THEY'LL ALWAYS WIN."

DID SOMETHING HAPPEN TODAY? AT SCHOOL?
OH... NO.

THIS DOESN'T HAVE ANYTHING TO DO WITH THAT GAME YOU'RE PLAYING, DOES IT?
It's a sign.
NO! NOT AT ALL. NO.
Micah hates you.

I JUST...I NEED TO STUDY.
Too late.
AH.
PROCRASTINATING. YOU'RE NOT SUPPOSED TO DO THAT, EITHER.
What's the use?
You're so weird.
I KNOW.

I'LL BE BACK TO CHECK ON YOU SHORTLY.
I'M GOING TO CALL DR. PENNY, SO WE CAN ADDRESS THIS IN YOUR NEXT SESSION.
OK.

OH YEAH, MOM, THERE WAS ONE MORE THING I WANTED TO--

--TELL YOU.

HELLO? DR. PENNY--OH MY, I APOLOGIZE. I THOUGHT I'D BE SENT TO VOICEMAIL.
YES, YES. WELL, I'M A BIT CONCERNED ABOUT ISAAC. HE--

SLAM

DRAMA!
FICTION!
FABLE! THRILLER!
FANTASY!
MYSTERY!

Forgot. You forgot everything.
You FORGET everything.
Sick. Stupid. Uneven. Dirty.

SQUEAK

READ FOR FUN!
FINISHED.
THANK YOU, MICAH.

IF YOU FINISH EARLY, FEEL FREE TO TAKE THE REST OF THE CLASS TO DO OTHER ASSIGNMENTS OR READ QUIETLY.
NO PHONES.
FINAL EXA

BZZZZZ

Give up.
You know that's wrong.
Do you, though? When you're wrong, you're right.
SQUEAK

BRRRRRRRRIINNNNNGGG

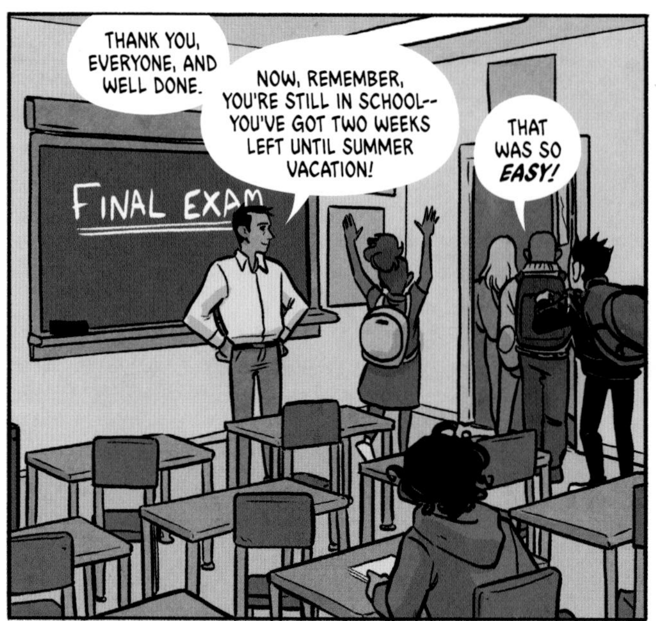
THANK YOU, EVERYONE, AND WELL DONE.
NOW, REMEMBER, YOU'RE STILL IN SCHOOL-- YOU'VE GOT TWO WEEKS LEFT UNTIL SUMMER VACATION!
THAT WAS SO ***EASY!***
FINAL EXAM

ISAAC?
HOW ARE WE DOING?

...
I'M DONE.
Stupid.
You probably have a brain disease.

PARTS of SPEECH
PRONOUN:
NOUN:
PROPER NOUN
VERB:
ADVERB:
PREPOSITION:
CONTRACTION:

You have a weird walk.
That's why you failed. Need to count steps.
READ For FU
ONE. TWO. THREE.

HEY.
YOU OK?
No.

YEAH. WELL...I DON'T THINK I DID GOOD ON THE TEST.
Pity.
AW MAN, I'M SORRY.
BUT I THINK IT HAPPENS TO EVERYONE.
They think you're stupid.

HAVE YOU EVER FAILED A TEST?
EHH...
I GOT A B MINUS ON A SPANISH QUIZ LAST QUARTER.
Dumb, stupid isaac.

...
Uneven. Sick.
HEY, DO YOU HAVE YOUR SKETCHBOOK ON YOU?

OH, YEAH.
BZZZ
COOOOOOOOL...
CAN I OPEN IT?
S-SURE.
Brain damage.
SKETCH!

WHOA!
SKETCH
IS THIS... SER BRIDGER LIGHTBORN?!
YEAH.
I THOUGHT IT WOULD BE FUN TO DRAW THEM.
IT'S AMAZING.
HMM...WANNA SIT OUTSIDE? IT'S REALLY NICE OUT.
WE HAD OUR ALGEBRA FINAL YESTERDAY, SO I HAVE THE PERIOD OFF.
ME TOO.
SKETCH

OHHH. I LOVE THIS ONE.
WHOA!
NOW YOU'RE JUST SHOWING OFF.
OH. I DIDN'T MEAN TO!
They hate you.
NO, I MEAN, YOU'RE JUST SO GOOD!
THIS SER BRIDGER LIGHTBORN...
HOW DID YOU GET THEM SO PERFECT?
IT'S LIKE YOU SAW WHAT I SAW. ARE YOU PSYCHIC OR SOMETHING?
HEH HEH--NO.
YOU SHOULD DRAW VOLIN, TOO.
REALLY?
ARE YOU KIDDING ME? YOU DEFINITELY SHOULD! SERIOUSLY, EVERY ONE OF THE CHARACTERS WOULD BE SO COOL--
BRRINNGG

ACK! GOTTA GO TO HISTORY.
WHAT DO YOU HAVE NEXT?
OH, UH. I HAVE AN APPOINTME--
I MEAN, I THINK I'LL STAY HERE FOR A BIT AND THEN GO TO THE CAFETERIA.

SEE YOU TOMORROW MORNING FOR MORE...
SWAMPS & SORCERY...

YEAH! SEE YA!

SKETCH!

ISAAC?
ISAAC
ITKIN?
HI. YEAH.
SORRY.
NOTHING
TO BE SORRY
FOR.
HAVE A
SEAT.
I'VE BEEN LOOKING
FORWARD TO
MEETING YOU.
YOU LIKE
TO DRAW?
DRAW?
OH. YEAH.
Tug your
ear.
THAT'S GREAT! WELL, YOU'RE
WELCOME TO DRAW AS
WE TALK.
REALLY?
Really?
ABSOLUTELY.
SOME PEOPLE THINK
BETTER WHEN THEY'RE
DRAWING. IT HELPS
THEM FOCUS.
SO, YOUR MOM
ALREADY TOLD ME
QUITE A BIT ABOUT
YOU.
THOUGH MOSTLY
SHE TALKED TO ME
ABOUT YOUR DIAGNOSIS
THIS YEAR. OBSESSIVE-
COMPULSIVE DISORDER,
SHE SAID.

WOULD YOU MIND TALKING TO ME ABOUT IT?
...OK.

I DID A LITTLE RESEARCH AND HAVE COME TO UNDERSTAND THAT HAVING OCD MEANS YOU HAVE TO DEAL WITH OBSESSIONS. THAT THEY MANIFEST AS UNWANTED URGES, IMAGES, AND THOUGHTS. AND THAT THEY LEAD TO DISTRESS, WHICH THEN LEAD TO COMPULSIONS.
DOES THAT SOUND RIGHT?
...MOSTLY.

MOSTLY?
WELL...I DON'T LIKE THE OBSESSIONS, AND THEY WON'T STOP COMING.
BUT I GUESS... WHAT I REALLY HATE IS THAT IT'S HARD TO KNOW WHERE THEY COME FROM.
HOW DO YOU MEAN?

IT'S LIKE...THEY'RE SCARY. I KNOW I'M NOT SUPPOSED TO TAKE THEM SERIOUSLY. MY DOCTOR ACTUALLY SAYS IT'S LIKE MY BRAIN IS LYING TO ITSELF.
BUT THEN, THEY ALSO COME FROM ME, RIGHT? AND I CAN'T STOP THINKING THAT ONLY BAD PEOPLE HAVE BAD THOUGHTS...
HMM...

WELL, WHAT ABOUT THAT, THERE?
WHAT?
Tug your ear.
THAT CREATURE YOU'RE DRAWING. A DRAGON, IT SEEMS LIKE.
YOU IMAGINED IT, RIGHT?

BUT IMAGINING IT DIDN'T PUT IT ON THE PAPER. TO DO THAT, YOU HAVE TO USE YOUR TALENT TO MAKE IT LOOK LIKE WHAT YOU'RE SEEING IN YOUR MIND.
WHY DO YOU CHOOSE TO DRAW THIS DRAGON INSTEAD OF, SAY, ONE OF THE OBSESSIVE THOUGHTS OR IMAGES THAT YOU DON'T LIKE?

MAYBE THIS IS WHAT REPRESENTS YOU INSTEAD. AND MAYBE YOUR BRAIN ISN'T LYING TO YOU AS MUCH AS IT'S A LITTLE TOO RECEPTIVE. LIKE AN ANTENNA THAT CATCHES TOO MANY SIGNALS AT ONCE.

YOU... THINK IT'S COOL?
IMAGINATION-BASED GAMES ARE SO INTRIGUING, AND I NEVER GOT TO TRY THEM MYSELF.
CAN YOU TELL ME MORE ABOUT WHO YOU'RE PLAYING WITH?
WELL, MY FRIENDS JAIME AND CARMEN, THEY'RE TWINS, YOU KNOW. AND CARMEN'S GOING TO BE LEADING THE GAME.
SHE'S REALLY SMART. LIKE, I'M PRETTY SURE SHE'S A GENIUS.
THIS IS MY FRIEND MICAH'S CHARACTER. THEY'RE A PALADIN.
I HAVE MY OWN CHARACTER. HE'S AN ELF.
AND HE'S FROM A PLACE CALLED THE LIBRARY OF MURMURS. MICAH TOLD ME I SHOULD DRAW HIM, TOO. I THINK I'LL DRAW ALL THE CHARACTERS.
AND ONE OF THE CHARACTERS IS NAMED GRUNTUS, BECAUSE ALL HE DOES IS GRUNT. AND THEN THERE'S BOBBERT.
BOBBERT?

BZZZ

Wizards.

I SUPPOSE I DID SAY THAT, MIRIAM. BUT I DIDN'T MEAN THAT ISAAC *CAN'T* READ FANTASY BOOKS.

BUT I DO THINK YOU SHOULD ASK YOURSELF IF READING SOMETHING LIKE THIS HELPS YOU IN ANY WAY. RATHER THAN SOMETHING BASED IN REALITY.
...OK.

WHATEVER. I'M GOING TO BED.
THIS EARLY?
Fried Milk

I SHOULD TAKE CARE OF A FEW THINGS BEFORE IT GETS TOO LATE.
SLAM
I'LL CHECK ON YOU LATER?
SURE.

OH, AND, MOM?
YES, DARLING?

CAN I...STAY FOR DINNER AT CARMEN AND JAIME'S TOMORROW?
...
DINNER?
the Wizard King Book 1

...
WHY?
IT WOULD BE FUN, I GUESS.
AND THEY INVITED ME.

WELL...I SUPPOSE THERE ISN'T AN ISSUE.
YES, OK. HAVE DINNER OVER AT YOUR FRIENDS' HOUSE TOMORROW.
MIRIAM AND I WILL COOK FOR TWO.

THANKS, MOM.
OF COURSE, DARLING.
JUST BE CAREFUL, OK?

I WILL.

"It's been an unusually cold month, particularly as Corvida's Notch is concerned.
"Travelers rarely require more than light silks in spring when traveling through this valley, but everyone you've crossed thus far has complained of an unnatural, winter~like chill.

THE PORKY SWALLOW
"Each of you adventurers ended up in Corvida's Notch for different reasons, but what you all have in common is that you're far from home, and you've come to rest at an inn called the Porky Swallow."

"Maybe it's the smell of the fireplace burning, or the mutton, mead, and revelry, but a calm sensation comes over you as you recall with fondness why you decided to set out on a journey to begin with."
WAIT, WHY *EXACTLY* DID I SET OUT ON A JOURNEY TO BEGIN WITH? I THINK I FORGOT MY ORIGIN STORY.
"Argh. You're a wandering musician trying to get a gig, Bobbert."
AH, RIGHT.
HELLO, MY GOOD BARKEEP.
WHAT'DYA WANT?
SQUIRK.
WELL, UH, THAT DEPENDS, WHAT'DYA GOT?
MENU'S ON THE WALL.
MENU
QUITE. HEY, YOU'RE NOT LOOKING TO HIRE A SUPER-METAL MUSICIAN BY ANY CHANCE, ARE YOU?
NO.
NOT A ROCKER, I SEE...

ANYTHING ELSE FOR YOU, SER?
...

WHAT'DYA WANT?
SQUIRK.
...

CONTEMPTUOUS BLASPHEMER...
YOU WILL COME WITH US IMMEDIATELY. I WOULD SAY THAT YOU SHOULD DO SO QUIETLY, BUT I'M NOT NAIVE ENOUGH TO EXPECT YOU WILL OBLIGE.

PATRONS! BY THE ORDER OF THE STEEL SUN, I DEMAND THAT YOU CLEAR THE PREMISES IMMEDIATELY!
WE HAVE BUSINESS TO ATTEND TO.

BUT WHERE WILL I SLEEP TONIGHT?
YEAH! I'VE ALREADY PAID FOR A HAYLOFT!
AND THIS STAG HEART'S DELICIOUS.
I SAID...
CLEAR THE PREMISES!

I DON'T WANT TO HAVE TO REPEAT MYSELF AGAIN...
I HEARD WHAT YOU SAID...

...BUT BY MY OATH TO CRUCAS THE PEACELORD, I CANNOT ALLOW YOU TO HARM ANYONE WITHOUT DUE CAUSE.

I HAVE CAUSE, PAGAN, BUT I WILL NOT BE SHARING IT WITH YOU.
GET THEM.

GRUNT!
MOMMY
CRASH

WOMMY
♫ YEAH, YEAH, WHAT?! WE'RE ♪ FIGHTING IN THE BAR ROOM!
♪ WHO KNEW ♫ THIS KINDA THING WOULD HAPPEN **SO SOON!**
WUMP

WHAT...
WHO?

BZZZT

WOW--
THAT WAS
WILD. REAL
WILD.
WHY
WERE THEY
OUT TO GET
YOU?

THEY
WEREN'T
AFTER THIS
WOMAN.
THEY
WERE AFTER
ME.
SQUIRK.

WAIT, WHAT DO YOU MEAN BY "ME"?
...
GRUNT?

TOMAS! HELP HINKLE GET THESE BRUTES INTO THE CELLAR BRIG.
AND GET EVERYONE ELSE A BEVERAGE OF THEIR CHOICE ON THE HOUSE.
HEY, ALL RIGHT!
AS FOR THE FIVE OF YOU, COME WITH ME...

IS THAT...?
DINNER!

AHEM! I SAID DINNER!
WE HEARD YOU!

NICE ILLUSION SPELL, ISAAC!
SERIOUSLY! WAS NOT EXPECTING THAT.
OH, UH, THANKS!
YOU ALL WERE SO GREAT, TOO.

YOU ALL COMING DOWN?

YES, YES, WE'RE DESCENDING TO DINE AT YOUR TABLE OF LIES.
OK, THEN.

AH! WELCOME!
I'VE MADE SOMETHING SPECIAL FOR YOU TODAY...

WEARY FROM THE ROAD, ADVENTURERS? GATHER ROUND, FOR TODAY'S SPECIAL INCLUDES A SPREAD SO HEARTY IT COULD PUT A DRAGON TO BED.
FIRST, WE HAVE MAXTARUS'S PIES, MADE FROM SPRING HARVEST VEGETABLES ENCHANTED BY NONE OTHER THAN THE WIZARD MAXTARUS OF CASTLE LINDONIA.
VEGETARIAN FRIENDLY.
SECOND!
MIST-MUSHROOM POTATO CHOWDER WITH FLAME-SEARED WYRM CRISPS. A GNOMISH SPECIALTY. BE SURE TO ASK FOR SECONDS.
AND THIRD! A DELICATE BREW FROM THE LANDS BEYOND, DANGEROUS IN SMALL QUANTITIES, HEALTHY IN LARGE ONES. IT IS CALLED...NECTARO!
AND IT HAS PINEAPPLE IN IT, IN CASE YOU'RE ALLERGIC TO PINEAPPLE.

WELL?
DIG IN!

DAD?
YES, CARE-BEAR?
THIS IS EXCEPTIONAL.

ISAAC, ARE YOU OK?

IT'S JUST SO... DELICIOUS.
HA HA HA!

NOAH, LESLIE--DO YOU LIKE TO COOK?
IT'S COOL, I GUESS. MY MOM TAUGHT ME HOW TO MAKE LUMPIA LAST WEEK.
I *LOVE* LUMPIA.
WHAT'S LUMPIA?

THEY'RE KIND OF LIKE EGG ROLLS BUT FILIPINO STYLE.
HUH. WELL, I HATE COOKING.
I LIKE EATING, THOUGH!

WHAT ABOUT YOU, ISAAC?
OH, UH, I DON'T KNOW.
Dumb. Uneven.
YOU DON'T KNOW IF YOU LIKE TO COOK?

I HAVEN'T TRIED BEFORE. MY MOM, SHE LIKES TO DO IT ALL.
I DON'T THINK SHE ASKS MY SISTER FOR HELP, EITHER.
IS THAT RIGHT?

WELL, MAYBE NEXT TIME YOU CAN COME OVER I CAN SHOW YOU A THING OR TWO?
REALLY?
OH, WE CAN MAKE EMPANADAS!
YEAH!

THAT SOUNDS GREAT.
You look sick.

WANNA SEE IT?
HUH?
IT'S MY MOM'S ART STUDIO.
OH. YEAH, OK.

SHE'S AN ILLUSTRATOR.
MOSTLY CHILDREN'S BOOKS, BUT OTHER STUFF, TOO.

I'M HAVING TROUBLE WITH THAT ONE.
EEP.

I JUST CAN'T FIGURE OUT HOW TO MAKE IT WORK.
THE STORY IS ABOUT A KID TRYING TO DELIVER A MESSAGE TO HIS FRIEND IN THE MIDDLE OF AN ENCHANTED STORM.
BEEN WORKING ON IT ALL MONTH.

IT'S...SO AMAZING.
WELL. IT'S GETTING THERE. I HOPE.

MOM, ISAAC LIKES TO DRAW, TOO. HE'S SUPER GOOD.
Good at having germs.
OH... UM...

IS THAT RIGHT?
WELL, IF YOU EVER WANT SOME TIPS AND TRICKS, LET ME KNOW. THE WORLD ALWAYS NEEDS MORE ARTISTS.

THAT WOULD BE AWESOME.
SEE YOU ALL LATER!
BZZ
OH, WE BETTER SAY GOODBYE TO NOAH.
SEE YA, KIDS.

SO, ISAAC, YOU'LL COME TO THE MIDNIGHT RELEASE WITH US?
A NEW ELI BOOK-- FINALLY!
Y-YEAH!
I MEAN, I HAVE TO ASK MY MOM, BUT I THINK SO.

YOU'RE *BIKING* HOME?
You don't have a bike.
Don't act nervous or they'll

OH, YEAH! I LIVE PRETTY CLOSE.
BUT... YOUR MOM LETS YOU?
Your fault.

TOTALLY! IT'S SAFE AROUND HERE, AND SHE KNOWS I'LL COME STRAIGHT HOME.
OH.

HEY...CAN I ASK YOU A QUESTION?
Y-YEAH.
Disgusting.
Tug again.
WHY DO YOU PULL YOUR EAR LIKE THAT?

Shame.
OH, UH...
They see you.
They know!
It's over.
I DIDN'T KNOW I WAS DOING THAT.

OH, GOTCHA. MUST HAVE BEEN CONFUSED.
I JUST, WELL, IT'S, LIKE, IF YOU, IT'S JUST NOT...

HEY.

IT'S NO PROBLEM. AT ALL.

I'LL SEE YOU ON MONDAY!
YEAH, SEE YOU!

OH, AND ISAAC?
HUH?

IF YOU EVER JUST WANT TO TALK TO ME, ABOUT ANYTHING, YOU KNOW...
I'M AROUND. ON MY OATH AS A KNIGHT OF CRUCAS.

...THANKS.

DARLING! OH MY, I HOPE YOU WEREN'T WAITING TOO LONG?
YOU'RE ALWAYS ON TIME.

WELL, MIRIAM AND I WENT OUT FOR DINNER, DIDN'T WE?
...WE GOT FAST FOOD AT STORMY'S.
I DECIDED NOT TO COOK FOR A CHANGE. AND AS FOR YOU? HOW WAS YOUR DINNER?
IT WAS REALLY GOOD.

HEY, MOM? MY FRIENDS--THEY'RE GOING TO A RELEASE EVENT AT THE TATTERED COVER FOR THE NEW ELI THE WIZARD KING BOOK NEXT WEEKEND.
AND THEY INVITED ME TO GO. CAN I?
IS THAT RIGHT? WELL, I DON'T SEE WHY NOT. WHAT TIME?

IT'S ON SATURDAY... AT MIDNIGHT.
MIDNIGHT?!
BUT JAIME AND CARMEN'S PARENTS WILL BE THERE.

I DON'T KNOW, ISAAC. I LOVE THAT YOU'RE MAKING FRIENDS, BUT THAT SOUNDS LIKE A LOT FOR YOU. AND ALL THIS MAKE-BELIEVE STUFF...
I PROMISE I'LL BE CAREFUL.

...FINE. BUT MIRIAM WILL GO WITH YOU.
Ugh. Not Miriam.
UGH. SERIOUSLY.
WHAT?! BUT I DON'T WANT TO GO TO SOME WEIRD FANTASY BOOK PARTY!
AND I HAVE PRACTICE THE NEXT DAY!
YES, IN THE AFTERNOON.

BESIDES. YOU DON'T SPEND ENOUGH TIME TOGETHER AS SIBLINGS. IT'LL BE GOOD FOR THE TWO OF YOU. I JUST KNOW IT.
BZZZ

BRRRRG

OOOOKAY. HERE ARE YOUR TESTS BACK.

Disaster. Failure.
Your fault.

A-MINUS!

A!

ROCKED IT.

You knew this would happen.

You got bad grades because you hate your mom.

You made friends so you would get bad grades.

EVIL

SOME SAY THAT EVERY PERSON IS A SUM OF THEIR PARTS, BUT THE ANIMALS OF PAW MEADOW WERE A SUM OF THEIR FARM...
A PIG WAS NOT JUST A PIG, BUT A PIG AND A DUCK AND A HORSE AND A COW.
PSST-- ISAAC?
CAFETERIA AFTER CLASS?
SURE.
IF HE STAYS HERE FOR LONG ENOUGH, HE THINKS THE REST OF PAW MEADOW WILL DISAPPEAR AS WELL.
Worthless.

OH YEAH...

WANT SOME? MY DAD MADE THEM.
OH, NO, I'M OK.
WANNA SEE SOMETHING, THOUGH?
BZZZ

WAAAAH!
BOBBERT!

DUDE. THIS. IS. SO DANK.
CARMEN IS GONNA FREAK.
FREAK, WILL I?

WAAAAH!
OK, YOU'RE RIGHT, I'M FREAKING!
I DID THE OTHERS, TOO.

GRUNTUS!
MOMMY

BZZ

SHADENOIR!

WHERE'S VOLIN?
I...I HAVEN'T DONE HIM YET.
I ANTICIPATE ITS COMPLETION.
OH, COOL.

SERIOUSLY, YOU'RE SO GOOD, ISAAC.
BROTHER, I NEED YOUR HELP CARRYING SOME PLANTS TO THE GREENHOUSE. IT'S FOR BIO.

BUH... FINE.
GOODBYE, ISAAC! UNTIL OUR PATHS MEET AGAIN. WHICH WILL BE SOON, AS PERTAINS TO US. AND AS PERTAINS TO PATHS.

BZZ

...failure.

You're a bad person.
D
see me to discuss
Describe the meaning of S

Disgusting.

THE
PORKY SWALLOW

IS THAT...?

YOU?

NO, *I* AM RIGHT HERE.
SHE IS TRAPPED IN THIS MIRROR OF ARCH-MIMICRY, BUT DON'T WORRY. SHE WON'T BE HARMED.

SO, LET ME GET THIS STRAIGHT. YOU, UH, WHATEVER YOU ARE--
CALL ME MOG.
YOU'RE SPEAKING THROUGH THIS IMPRISONED BARKEEP?

IF THAT'S THE CASE, I CANNOT ABIDE SUCH LAWLESSNESS.

SHE IS NOT A BARKEEP.

SHE IS A SORCERESS, AND SHE TRAPPED ME TO BEGIN WITH FOR THE SAME REASONS THAT BAND OF ACOLYTES CAME AFTER ME EARLIER.

BECAUSE I'M THE ONLY WAY THEY'RE GOING TO FIND THE ***TOWER OF GREENMOON.***

WHAT'S THE TOWER OF GREENMOON?

AHA! HERE IT IS...

"HOME TO THE EMERALD EMPRESS, THE TOWER OF GREENMOON WAS ONCE A SOURCE OF GREAT POWER.

"RUN BY A SOCIETY OF WIZARDS, IT WAS THOUGHT TO HAVE VANISHED LONG AGO WHEN THE STEEL QUEEN BEGAN HER CONQUEST OF RIZULEA.

ink

"SOME SPECULATE THAT IT WAS RAZED DURING THESE WARS, THOUGH NO ACTUAL ACCOUNTS OF THIS EXIST."

THAT'S BECAUSE IT DIDN'T OCCUR.
THE STEEL QUEEN SOUGHT OUT THE TOWER OF GREENMOON AS A SOURCE OF POWER. SHE KNEW THAT IF SHE COULD HARNESS THE WIZARDS' SECRETS, SHE WOULD BECOME UNSTOPPABLE.

WHEN THE WIZARDS OF GREENMOON UNDERSTOOD THESE AIMS, THEY CAST A VERY POWERFUL SPELL TO HIDE THE TOWER ON ANOTHER ASTRAL PLANE.
BUT SINCE THE MAGIC WAS SO STRONG, IT STILL REMAINS THERE TO THIS DAY...WITH LITTLE ABILITY TO RETURN.

I WAS SENT TO THIS PLANE TO DELIVER A WAY FOR THE TOWER'S RETURN, SHOULD THOSE WORTHY OF SUCH A QUEST BE FOUND.

SO, YOU ARE THE KEY TO FINDING THE TOWER.
CORRECT, KNIGHT.
AND IF THE STEEL QUEEN HAS HER WAY, SHE'LL USE ME TO FIND THE TOWER, KILL THOSE INSIDE, AND BLEED IT OF ITS ANCIENT MAGIC. THE TERRORS SHE WILL THEN UNLEASH...THEY CHILL THE SOUL.

SO WHY DID YOU BRING US IN HERE, THEN? TELL US ALL THIS? HOW DO YOU KNOW WE WON'T TAKE YOU STRAIGHT TO THE STEEL QUEEN HERSELF?
BECAUSE...

...THE MOMENT YOU HELPED ME, YOU WERE CHOSEN BY THE EMERALD EMPRESS.
DON'T BELIEVE ME? LOOK AROUND YOUR NECKS.
GRUNT?!

RINGS. WHERE DID THESE COME FROM?
THEY AREN'T JUST RINGS... NO.

EACH OF YOU
OW BEARS THE
MBODIED SPIRIT
F A WIZARD OF
GREENMOON.
I'VE CARRIED THEM WITH ME IN THE HOPE THAT SOMEONE WOULD PROVE WORTHY ENOUGH TO JOURNEY INTO THE TOWER AND BRING IT BACK TO THIS PLANE.

WHEN YOU CHOSE TO HELP ME, IT SO HAPPENED THAT THEY MADE THE DECISION TO BOND TO YOU.

I'VE HEARD OF THIS PHENOMENON AS WELL. ANCIENT MAGIC, LITTLE PRACTICED ANYMORE. TOO COMPLICATED FOR MODERN MAGES.
CORRECT.
THIS IS KINDA DOPE.

WHAT ARE WE MEANT TO DO WITH THESE?
MEANT? I CANNOT BE SURE.
BUT WHAT WE MUST DO IS JOURNEY EAST--TO THE CAVERN OF FORGOTTEN MEMORIES.
NICE.

THERE, EACH OF YOU SHALL BE CHALLENGED TO FACE YOUR FEARS AS A TEST FOR ENTERING THE TOWER OF GREENMOON.
NOT SO NICE.

AND WHAT IF WE CHOOSE NOT TO GO, EH? I'M TRUE NEUTRAL, AND I SAY, WHAT DO I GET OUT OF JOINING THIS QUEST?

IT'S NOT SO MUCH A MATTER OF WHAT YOU'LL RECEIVE...AS WHAT WILL HAPPEN TO YOU IF YOU CHOOSE TO WALK AWAY.
YOU HAVE BEEN SELECTED BY GREENMOON NOW. AND IF YOU REFUSE THE CALL, IT WILL BECOME A CURSE.

GRR...I DON'T LIKE THIS.
I THINK WE SHOULD GO.

WE CAN'T CHOOSE OUR DESTINY.
BUT ONCE IT'S PART OF US, WE CAN'T IGNORE IT, EITHER. AND SHOULDN'T.
THE QUEST WE'VE BEEN CHOSEN FOR... MAYBE IT'S NOT A CURSE. MAYBE THE WIZARDS OF GREENMOON SAW SOMETHING INSIDE US THAT...THAT WE COULDN'T SEE INSIDE OURSELVES.

SOMETHING GOOD. AND STRONG.

I WILL JOURNEY TO THE TOWER OF GREENMOON. I HOPE THE REST OF YOU WILL AS WELL.

GRUNT!
HEAR, HEAR!
HEAR, HEAR!
UGH. FINE.

"SO IT'S DECIDED," MOG SAYS, THROUGH THE VOICE OF THE OLD WOMAN. "WE SET OUT TOMORROW AT DAWN."
GRUNT! IT'S 4:30!

REALLY? I WISH WE COULD KEEP PLAYING.
YEAH, ME TOO.
OH, HEY, I ALMOST FORGOT!

MY MOM'S TAKING ME CAMPING IN A FEW WEEKENDS, AND I THINK IT FALLS ON A SWAMPS & SORCERY DAY. SO, I WAS THINKING...
YOU ALL WANT TO COME?
CAMPING?
LIKE, WITH BEARS AND STUFF?

YEP! WELL, NO--NO BEARS. BUT S'MORES, CAMPFIRE, STARS, ALL THAT STUFF.
WE GO EVERY YEAR, SOMETIMES WITH OTHER FAMILY FRIENDS.
INTERESTING... DO YOU THINK MY PARENTS COULD COME, TOO, IF THEY WANTED?
OF COURSE!

SWAMPS & SORCERY...IN THE FOREST...
HECK YES!
ISAAC? WHAT ABOUT YOU?
THAT...SOUNDS AWESOME.
D

I NEED TO ASK MY MOM, THOUGH. I'VE NEVER BEEN CAMPING BEFORE --OOF!
Germs. Sick.
You don't deserve to go.
MY DUDE, IT'S THE ABSOLUTE BEST.

HA HA--
HONK
OH, THAT'S MY MOM. GOTTA GO.

SEE YOU, ISAAC!
SEE YOU!
SAFE JOURNEYS, MASTER VOLIN!

...

HI, MOM.
HI, DARLING.

HOW ABOUT WE LISTEN TO SOME MUSIC?
OK.

Failure.

AN A-***PLUS?***
WOW, MIRIAM! AND THIS IS ALGEBRA, RIGHT?
BZZZ
PHYSICS! BUT STILL, IT WAS REALLY HARD.

YOU KNOW, YOU'RE GOING TO BE ABLE TO START THINKING OF WHERE YOU WANT TO GO TO SCHOOL SOON.
I'M ALREADY IN SCHOOL.
I MEAN COLLEGE, MIRIAM.

OH, YEAH. WELL, I WAS TALKING TO HEIDI, YOU KNOW, MY FRIEND FROM THE VOLLEYBALL TEAM, AND ***SHE*** SAID SHE MIGHT APPLY TO STATE--
ISAAC, DARLING! COME AND HAVE A SEAT.

TELL ME ABOUT THIS WEEK'S MEETING WITH MR. BODUM, DARLING.
BUT I ALREADY TOLD YOU.
I KNOW. BUT I WANT TO HEAR IT AGAIN. IT'S IMPORTANT TO ME.
I'M NOT IMPORTANT TO YOU.

WELL, HE WAS REALLY NICE.
HE LET ME DRAW DURING THE SESSION.
IS THAT RIGHT?

WHAT DID HE SAY?
WE TALKED ABOUT MY OCD FOR A LITTLE WHILE.
IT'S HARD TO, UH, EXPLAIN.

OH, THAT'S OK, NO BOTHER. I'D LIKE TO MEET HIM, THOUGH.
OK.
AHEM!

YES, MIRIAM.
NEVER MIND.

PUT YOUR PLATE--
IN THE SINK. YEAH.

HOW IS THAT BROCCOLI? I PUT CHEDDAR ON IT.
Separate the food.

...
MR. ITKIN! I SEE YOU HAVEN'T A COSTUME.

I STILL CAN'T BELIEVE YOU DRAGGED ME TO THIS.
I DIDN'T. MOM SAID YOU HAD TO COME.
SAME THING.
EVERYONE, CHECK THIS OUT!

EL: the WIZARD KING
BOOK 3

THE LINE'S MOVING!
ISAAC? ARE YOU EXCITED?

FORGIVE ME IF I'M MISTAKEN, BUT YOU'RE ON THE VOLLEYBALL TEAM, ARE YOU NOT?
UH, NO. I MEAN, YEAH. I AM.
HOW COMPELLING. I PERSONALLY DON'T HAVE A PENCHANT FOR TEAM SPORTS, BUT I DO APPRECIATE ATHLETICISM.

HAVE YOU EVER PLAYED *BLOOD YETI'S BETRAYAL*?
NO.
ISAAC, ISAAC. WHAT'DYA THINK ABOUT THE ENDING OF BOOK TWO?
AAH!
I CAN'T BELIEVE ELI WENT OVER TO PROWLER.

I DECIDE WHO IS A WIZARD AND WHO IS NOT!

K.J. PROWLER! CAN WE HAVE A PICTURE?
PLEASE?

YOU'RE SO GOOD AT LOOKING HORRIBLE!
THANK YOU.

TONIGHT, WE HAVE THE ABSOLUTE HONOR OF HOSTING TANIA FORD, FOR THE RELEASE OF HER NEWEST ENTRY IN THE INTERNATIONALLY BESTSELLING SERIES, ***ELI THE WIZARD KING: PROWLER'S CHALLENGE!***
CLAP
CLAP
CLAP
CLAP

CLAP CLAP CLAP
CLAP CLAP
CLAP
THE TATTERED COVER

CLAP CLAP CLAP
CLAP CLAP

THANK YOU SO MUCH, ALL OF YOU.
NOT A LOT OF YOU KNOW THIS, BUT DENVER IS MY HOMETOWN. SO I'M REALLY HONORED TO BE BACK. I PRACTICALLY GREW UP AT THIS BOOKSTORE, WHEN IT USED TO BE IN A DIFFERENT PART OF TOWN.
THE TATTERED COVER

BUT I'LL BEGIN AT THE BEGINNING, AND END SOON AFTER THAT, BEING THAT IT'S LATE AND I SEE A LOT OF KIDS IN THE AUDIENCE WHO DRAGGED THEIR PARENTS HERE AT THE STROKE OF MIDNIGHT.
I CAME VOLUNTARILY!
DAD!
HA HA HA! WELL, THAT'S A GOOD THING.
SEE, I GREW UP IN A HOME WHERE WHAT YOU'RE DOING RIGHT NOW WASN'T ENCOURAGED--OR EVEN ALLOWED, IN SOME CASES.

WHAT I MEAN IS, EXPRESSING YOURSELVES.
DRESSING UP. MAKING YOUR DREAMS--AND MINE--COME TO LIFE.

THANKFULLY, WHEN I WAS AROUND THE AGE MANY OF YOU IN THE AUDIENCE ARE RIGHT NOW, MY AUNT, A WOMAN WHO'S VERY SPECIAL TO ME, STARTED TO DO AN INCREDIBLY WONDERFUL THING.
SNEAK ME BOOKS.

AND EVENTUALLY, THOSE BOOKS LED TO ME WANTING TO WRITE BOOKS MYSELF. NOT JUST BECAUSE I ENJOYED STORIES.
BUT BECAUSE I WANTED TO CREATE THE KIND OF WORLD I NEEDED WHEN I WAS A CHILD.
BZZ

THERE ARE A LOT OF BIG STORIES IN THE WORLD TODAY. SOME OF THEM ARE SO BIG THEY LEAD TO MOVIES, TOYS, AND EVEN AMUSEMENT PARKS.
I STILL CAN'T BELIEVE ELI IS ON ITS WAY UP THERE. BECAUSE IT IS, AND IT'S SUPER WEIRD. AND BECAUSE OF ALL THAT, I WANT YOU ALL TO KNOW...

...UNLIKE WITH SOME STORIES ABOUT MAGIC, ELI BELONGS TO YOU.

CLAP
CLAP
CLAP
CLAP
CLAP

REMEMBER, ONE QUESTION EACH! NEXT!

MY DELIGHT KNOWS NO END, MS. FORD. MY NAME IS CARMEN. CARMEN LINDO.
AND I AM CONFIDENT IN MY ASSERTION THAT I'M, QUANTITATIVELY, IN FACT, YOUR MOST ENGAGED FAN.
WELL, THAT'S WONDERFUL!
WHUMP
IT IS. NOW, I ASSUME I CAN STILL ASK A QUESTION, IF YOUR OFFER STILL STANDS?

WHAT AM I GOING TO ASK HER?
ASK HER WHY I CAN'T BE AT HOME RIGHT NOW.
...AND *IF* IT'S A LOGICAL FALLACY, THEN IS ELI'S QUEST PARADOXICAL IN ITS VERY NATURE?
UM.

SAGACIOUS ANSWER!
WHY, HELLO THERE.

H-HI.
Uneven. Crooked.
I REALLY LOVE YOUR BOOKS.
AW. I'M SO GLAD TO HEAR THAT. AND WHAT'S YOUR NAME?

...
FOR THE SIGNATURE.
OH. ISAAC.
Germs.

WHAT A GREAT NAME.
Dear Isaac,
This story belongs to you.
Splendidly,
Tania Ford

WELL, HERE YOU ARE, ISAAC. I HOPE IT BRINGS YOU JOY.
DID YOU WANT TO ASK ME A QUESTION?
OH, UH...

...
WHY DO YOU THINK YOUR AUNT DECIDED TO SNEAK YOU BOOKS?
Stupid question.

HUH. I DON'T THINK ANYONE'S ASKED ME THAT BEFORE...

WHEN SOMEONE REALLY CARES ABOUT YOU, I THINK THEY SEE THE BEST VERSION OF WHO YOU ARE OR CAN BE.
I THINK MY AUNT SAW SOMETHING VALUABLE IN ME, BUT ALSO KNEW THAT SHE'D HAVE TO INTERVENE TO HELP ME SEE IT AS WELL.

THAT'S WHAT I LIKE TO THINK, ANYWAY. AND I'M GLAD FOR IT.
...THANK YOU, MS. FORD.
Diseased.
OF COURSE.
UM, ISAAC? ONE MOMENT, IF YOU DON'T MIND.

TAKE THIS.
IT'S A SPECIAL PEN THAT I USE FOR WRITING. THEY DON'T MAKE THEM ANYMORE, SO THERE ARE ONLY A FEW LEFT.
R-REALLY? BUT I COULDN'T. ESPECIALLY IF--

I WON'T HEAR ANOTHER WORD.
BUT... ARE YOU SURE?

I AM.
I DON'T KNOW WHY, BUT I SENSE YOU'RE THE KIND OF PERSON WHO JUST...NEEDS A SPECIAL PEN.

SHE GAVE YOU SOMETHING?
WHAT IS IT?
BZZ

SHE SAID IT'S A SPECIAL PEN. THERE AREN'T THAT MANY LEFT.
WHOA. AND SHE JUST GAVE IT TO YOU?
YEAH. I DIDN'T ASK OR ANYTHING.

WHAT ARE YOU GOING TO DO WITH IT? DRAW? START A JOURNAL?
SEQUESTER IT BEHIND AIR-PROOF GLASS?

CAN I...YOUR HAND?
OH, SURE.

THE SIGIL OF GREENMOON!

DO ME NEXT!
AND THEN ME!
OK.
HEY!

IT'S ALMOST 1:30 IN THE MORNING. WE NEED TO GET HOME.
...
YEAH, YOU'RE PROBABLY RIGHT. IT IS LATE.
AWWWW...

Tattere
ARE YOU... OK?
HOW CAN YOU EVEN ASK THAT QUESTION?
HUH?
Stupid.

EVERYONE IS ALWAYS WORRYING ABOUT YOU. PAYING SO MUCH ATTENTION. MEANWHILE? WHERE AM I?
STUCK HERE DOING THE SAME THING. UGH.

OH, THERE'S MY MOM! OK, SEE YOU ALL LATER.
WE'RE GOING WITH THEM!
SLEEPOVER!
BYE!

...DARLING?
BZZ

ISAAC?
HUH!

OH, SORRY. THE BOOK.
I CAN SEE THAT. IT'S QUITE IMMERSIVE, IS IT?
WHAT IS THAT?
OH. JUST A...PEN.
YOU'RE NOT GOING TO TELL HER, ISAAC?

MIRIAM? WHAT ARE YOU TALKING ABOUT?
THE AUTHOR OF THE BOOK HE'S READING, SHE GAVE IT TO HIM AS A SPECIAL GIFT.
APPARENTLY, THEY DON'T MAKE THEM ANYMORE.

OH. WHY DIDN'T YOU TELL ME ABOUT THAT, DARLING?
I WAS--I WAS GOING TO. I JUST FORGOT BECAUSE I WAS READING.
AH. I UNDERSTAND.
REALLY, MOM? YOU UNDERSTAND?

DO YOU ALSO UNDERSTAND THAT ISAAC GOT A D ON HIS LITERATURE TEST LAST WEEK?
WHAT?

I SAW YOU LOOKING AT IT IN THE CAFETERIA, ISAAC. YOU GOT A D. AND YOU HID IT FROM MOM.
ISAAC... IS THIS TRUE?
HE SAID I COULD RETAKE IT.

IT'S THIS--IT'S THIS GROUP, ISN'T IT? THESE GAMES?
I KNEW IT WAS A MISTAKE FOR YOU TO GET INVOLVED. I KNEW YOU WOULD BECOME DISTRACTED.
Death!
MOM, NO! IT'S NOT THE GAME. IT'S JUST...
Sick!

WHAT IS IT, THEN?
PLEASE DON'T MAKE ME STOP PLAYING! PLEASE?!
Sick.
Uneven.
Stupid.
Ugly.
Germs.
They hate you!

I WANT YOU TO FIGURE OUT HOW TO GET YOUR GRADE UP IN THAT CLASS.
IF YOU DON'T? THEN I WILL NOT ONLY FORBID YOU FROM PLAYING THE GAME, BUT YOU WILL STOP SEEING THOSE KIDS FOR GOOD. DO YOU UNDERSTAND?

WHY DO YOU... HATE ME SO MUCH?

Ser Bridger Lightborn

MASTER VOLIN!
...HEY.
HEY! ARE YOU OK?

YEAH. JUST CALLING TO SAY... HI.
WELL, *HI!* I WAS JUST ABOUT TO TEXT YOU, ACTUALLY.
YOU WANNA HEAD OUT TO RUBIX'S WITH ME, LESLIE, AND NOAH FOR ICE CREAM? THEY HAVE THE WEIRDEST FLAVORS.

OH, I CAN'T. I HAVE TO STUDY.
FOR WHAT? AREN'T FINALS OVER?
MR. DELAQUA'S GOING TO LET ME RETAKE THE TEST.

THAT'S SO COOL HE'S LETTING YOU RETAKE IT! BUT SAD YOU'RE STUCK AT HOME.
ICE CREAM SHALL BE EATEN IN YOUR HONOR, I SUPPOSE.
YEAH. HEH. THANKS.
TALK TO YOU SOO--
CLICK

Call ended

"The Jokeless Woods seem to wind indefinitely, and, honoring their namesake, are drabber and more mirthless than any other you've encountered."

THE ENTRANCE TO THE CAVERN OF FORGOTTEN MEMORIES SHOULD BE CLOSE.
SOON, WE WILL CONFRONT ITS MYRIAD OF DANGERS.
NICE. CAN'T WAIT.

WORRY NOT, BOBBERT. WE'VE THE SHIELD OF CRUCAS TO PROTECT US.
YEAH, I GUESS THAT'S TRUE.

MAYBE I CAN CAST A FINDING SPELL AND--
AHA! HERE IT IS!
THE ENTRANCE!

WELL DONE, BRIDGER.
YES, WELL DONE.
GRUNT.

WE MAY HAVE REACHED THE ENTRANCE, BUT THAT DOESN'T MEAN WE'VE GAINED ENTRY.
GRUNT?

GRUUUUUUUUNNNTTZZZZZZ
GRUNTUS! DO YOU NEED HEALING?
THE CAVERN OF FORGOTTEN MEMORIES WON'T LET YOU IN WITHOUT A SACRIFICE.
GRUNT.
...WHAT KIND OF SACRIFICE?

A MEMORY.
NOT OF YOUR CHOOSING, BUT TAKEN AS A SACRIFICE FOR THE CAVERN, IN EXCHANGE FOR PASSAGE.

IS THERE NO WAY AROUND IT?
I WILL CHECK MY BOOK.
...

HMM...MAYBE IF I CAST...NO. NO. THAT WON'T WORK.
CAVERN OF FORGOTTEN MEMORIES!
I IMPLORE YOU TO TAKE ONE OF MY MEMORIES, AN IMPORTANT ONE, AS TRIBUTE FOR ALL OF US!

UNNNNGHHH...

SER BRIDGER, ARE YOU OK?
WHAT MEMORY DID THEY TAKE?
UNGH...YES. YES, I AM.
I...DON'T KNOW...
LOOK, THE BARRIER IS DOWN!

YOU SACRIFICED ONE OF YOUR DEAREST MEMORIES SO NONE OF US HAD TO? HOW BRAVE.
THAT WAS HARDCORE.
WORRY NOT, FRIENDS. I HAVE MEMORIES TO SPARE.

♫ SER BRIDGER ♪ LIGHTBORN!
THE HERO WE NEED!
THE HERO WE YEARN FOR! ♫
THEY'RE ♪ A HERO MACHINE!
...

I THINK I FOUND A WAY WE COULD HAVE MADE IT PAST WITHOUT ANYONE LOSING THEIR MEMORIES.
HERO ♫ MACHINE!

IMPS!

WELL DONE, SER BRIDGER! YET AGAIN, YOUR HEROISM PRECEDES YOU.
AH, WELL.
♫ HEROISM PRECEDES YOU!
IT MEANS ♪ WHAT IT MEANS!
AND THAT IS THAT, YES, YOU ♫ ARE A HERO MACHINE! ♪

♫ HERO MACHINE!

♪ HERO MACHINE!

HERO ♫ MACHINE!

WELL, I COULD HAVE HELPED. USED MAGIC, FOR ONE.

YOU DON'T HAVE TO...HAVE--HAVE TO SAVE US ALL THE TIME, YOU KNOW?

HUH?

I...

Stupid. Selfish. Sick.

They're better than you.

VOLIN, ARE YOU OK?

Weird.

Uneven.

They pity you.

Sick!

YO!
ISAAC!

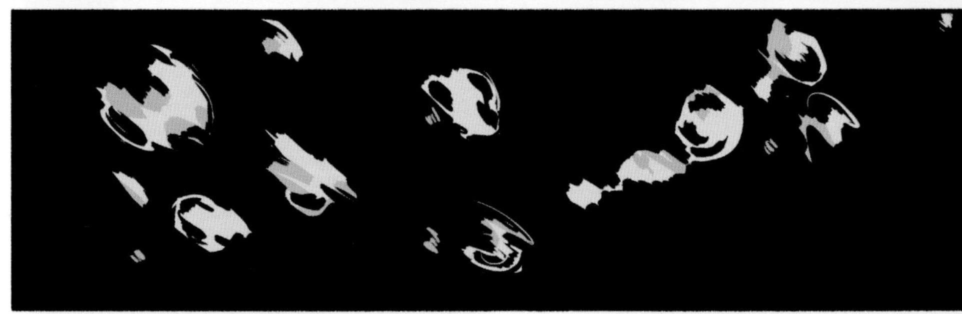

HEY.
ARE YOU OK?

YEAH... NO...I DON'T KNOW. I HAVE PROBLEMS, I THINK.
WHAT KIND?

I HAVE...I HAVE THIS THING. OCD...
OCD? WHAT'S THAT?
IT'S HARD TO EXPLAIN...IT'S, LIKE, I CAN'T STOP SEEING MYSELF IN THE WRONG WAY. BECAUSE OF THESE...

I THINK MY SISTER HATES ME. AND, IT'S, LIKE...I'M NOT TRYING TO HURT PEOPLE, BUT I'M AWFUL AND I DO IT ANYWAY, AND THEY HATE ME.
OH.
...

MICAH...EVERYONE LIKES YOU. YOU'RE JUST...YOU'RE SO SOLID, I GUESS.
WHAT IS IT LIKE? TO BE THAT WAY?
...I DON'T KNOW WHAT YOU MEAN.

YOU'RE NICE. AND YOU'RE... SO GOOD TO TALK TO. AND SMART. AND YOU SEEM LIKE YOU REALLY LIKE BEING AROUND ME.

AND I DON'T KNOW WHY THAT IS. BECAUSE I FEEL LIKE NO ONE SHOULD WANT TO BE AROUND ME. LIKE I'M...

Sick.

Weird.

Uneven.

SO weird.

THE THING IS, ISAAC...I DO REALLY LIKE YOU.
ALL OF US DO.
...REALLY?
YEAH. OF COURSE.

WHY, THOUGH?
WHY?
THAT'S A HARD QUESTION.

WITH YOU, I GUESS I'D SAY IT'S MORE THAN JUST A FEELING. BECAUSE THE MORE I, UH, CARE...ABOUT YOU, THE MORE I SEE...
GOODNESS... CREATIVITY...SO MUCH THOUGHTFULNESS...

MY MOM ONCE SAID THAT WHEN YOU CARE ABOUT SOMEONE, YOU SEE GOOD THINGS THAT SOMETIMES THEY CAN'T EVEN SEE IN THEMSELVES.
MAYBE THAT'S WHY.

HEY! I GOT SOME HOMEMADE DOUGHNUTS HERE! *WHOOOOOO* WANTS SOME?
DOUGHNUTS?!

SO YOU LEFT THE GROUP IN THE MIDDLE OF THE GAME?
YEAH...

I THINK BECAUSE, WELL, MICAH...IT'S LIKE EVERYONE LOVES THEM, YOU KNOW?
ACTUALLY, I DON'T. CAN YOU ELABORATE?

THEY'RE JUST SO EASY TO TALK TO. AND REAL. AND NICE. SO, THERE'S NOT ANYTHING WRONG WITH THEM AT ALL.

I'M AFRAID I DON'T FOLLOW. THIS IS THEIR CHARACTER IN THE GAME?
NO. NOT JUST THE GAME. BUT IN REAL LIFE. IT'S JUST...WHO THEY ARE.
AND WHY DOES THAT UPSET YOU?

IT DOESN'T.

I MEAN, I GUESS IT DOES.
WHY WOULD MICAH BEING A GOOD PERSON UPSET YOU?
WELL, I TOLD YOU ABOUT MY THOUGHTS. HOW THEY MAKE ME FEEL...
Disgusting.
...BAD. ABOUT WHO I AM.

SO I WONDER WHY SOMEONE LIKE MICAH WOULD LIKE ME. AND I WONDER WHY I CAN'T LOOK AT MYSELF IN THE SAME WAY THAT THEY SEE ME. OR THAT THEY SEE THEM.
...

THAT'S REALLY PERCEPTIVE OF YOU, ISAAC. THAT YOU SEE THAT AT ALL.
MOST PEOPLE DON'T SPEND THEIR TIME THINKING ABOUT THEMSELVES AND OTHERS SO THOROUGHLY.
FUEL

IT'S NOT BAD FOR YOU TO THINK ABOUT WHY MICAH CHOSE YOU AS A FRIEND.
BUT IT'S GOOD TO KNOW THAT YOU ALSO CHOSE TO BE FRIENDS WITH THEM. ALL RELATIONSHIPS ARE A TWO-WAY STREET.

IS THAT ANOTHER CHARACTER FROM THE GAME?
YEAH. SHE'S AN OLD WOMAN. BUT SHE'S ALSO A FLOATING OCTOPUS.
CLEARLY.
IT SOUNDS LIKE YOU'LL BE KEPT BUSY PLAYING STRAIGHT THROUGH THE SUMMER.

BZZ
YEAH... IF MY MOM LETS ME.

WHY WOULDN'T SHE LET YOU?
A TEST GRADE.
A BAD ONE.
Crooked.

MR. DELAQUA SAID I COULD RETAKE IT. BUT MY MOM TOLD ME THAT IF I DO BAD AGAIN, I HAVE TO QUIT THE GROUP.
I THINK SHE THINKS...THE GAME IS BAD FOR ME. FOR MY OCD.

I'M GLAD YOU'RE ALLOWED TO RETAKE THE TEST.
AND EVEN MORE SO, TO BE HONEST, I HOPE YOU CONTINUE ON WITH SWAMPS & SORCERY.
REALLY? ...WHY?
FUEL

I THINK IT'S GOOD FOR YOU. I'LL JUST SAY THAT FOR NOW.
YOUR MOM-- SHE CARES A LOT FOR YOU. THAT'S WHY SHE'S PROTECTIVE. BUT THAT DOESN'T MEAN THAT SHE UNDERSTANDS WHY CERTAIN THINGS ARE SO IMPORTANT TO YOU RIGHT NOW.

BUT THEN... WHAT SHOULD I DO? IF SHE SAYS I CAN'T PLAY?
I CAN'T ANSWER THAT, ISAAC.
BUT I CAN SAY THAT I THINK YOUR BIGGEST HURDLE WILL BE LEARNING TO TRUST YOURSELF.

AND I KNOW YOU CAN OVERCOME IT.

SKETCH!

I THOUGHT WE AGREED YOU'D RECEIVE A BETTER TEST GRADE BEFORE YOU WENT ON THIS... OVERNIGHT.
YOU WEREN'T FIBBING, WERE YOU?
She hates you.
NO, MOM. I PROMISE.

I TOOK THE TEST YESTERDAY.
BZZZ
MR. DELAQUA SAID HE'LL GET THE NEW GRADE TO ME ON MONDAY.
EVEN THOUGH SUMMER VACATION STARTS TODAY?
YES.

OH! THEY'RE HERE!
OK. OK. HAVE A...GOOD TIME. BE CAREFUL.
YOU'LL HAVE CELL PHONE SERVICE, IF YOU NEED IT?

BYE!
MIRIAM, SAY GOODBYE TO YOUR BROTHER.
SLAM
BYE.

Count the road lines.
Can't see them?
You'll make the car crash.

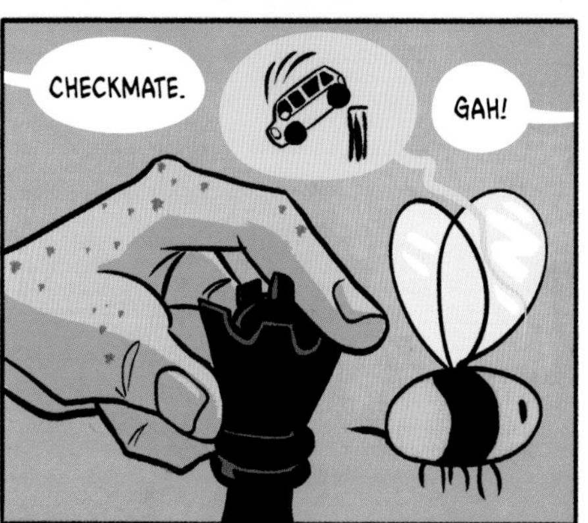
CHECKMATE.
GAH!

AGAIN, IN THREE MOVES! HOW?!
THEY KEEP GETTING YOU ON FOOL'S MATE! CAREFUL NOT TO TAKE THE BAIT.

DO YOU PLAY CHESS A LOT, MRS. PETERSEN?
ALICE. AND YES, I DO. KIND OF A TRADITION IN OUR FAMILY.
MY GRANDPA PLAYED PROFESSIONALLY.
SERIOUSLY?

YEP. HE WAS KINDA FAMOUS, TOO.
WELL, FAMOUS AMONG CHESS PEOPLE.
RIGHT.

I WANT TO LEARN HOW TO PLAY...
WELL, I'LL TEACH YOU WHEN WE GET TO THE CAMPSITE. THEN YOU AND JAIME CAN FACE OFF. MIGHT BE A FAIRER MATCH.
WHAT'S THE CAMPSITE LIKE WHERE WE'RE GOING TO?
PFF.
Weird voice.

OH, THAT'S RIGHT--YOU'VE NEVER BEEN BEFORE.
YOU'RE GONNA LOVE IT SO MUCH.
I'VE ONLY SEEN PICTURES, BECAUSE WE HAVEN'T BEEN TO THIS ONE BEFORE--BUT THERE ARE WOODS AND MOUNTAINS AND EVEN A LAKE.

SWAMPS & SORCERY, S'MORES, SAUSAGES, STARS. SICK.
ALSO, ALL WORDS THAT START WITH S.
YOU KIDS CAN OPEN THE WINDOWS IF YOU WANT. IT'S A BEAUTIFUL DAY.

SAN ISABEL
National
Forest

LOOK AT THIS PLACE!
IT'S PRETTIER THAN I EXPECTED.

HI, CARMEN!
FIRST THINGS FIRST.

OUR REGENTS WILL SURELY BE PREPARING VICTUALS FOR US SHORTLY.
VICTUALS?
LUNCH. SHE'S TALKING ABOUT LUNCH.

AFTER CONSUMING THEM, I BELIEVE WE'RE SCHEDULED TO TOUR THE LOCAL WILDS.
WHICH MEANS THAT NOW IT WOULD BEHOOVE US TO STAKE OUT TERRITORY IN WHICH SWAMPS & SORCERY WILL RECOMMENCE.
WHO WILL AID ME?

I GOT THE COOLER!
GREAT! I'LL HELP MAX WITH THE STOVE.

HOW ABOUT HERE?
WELL. IT'S FLAT. FEW PINE CONES. NICE, SOFT GROUND, AND ADEQUATE SURFACES.
IT'S DECIDED.

BZZZZZ
SWAMPS & SORCERY

sPlip
Plip
Plip
Plip

I THINK WE'RE GETTING NEAR THE TOWER.

YOU REALLY THINK SO? I CAN'T BELIEVE IT.

I WANT TO SEE WHAT THAT TALISMAN DOES.

ACTUALLY, I MIGHT BE ABLE TO FIGURE IT OUT WITH A SPELL. I JUST LEVELED UP!

IT'S OK. THEY'RE JUST HONEYBEES.
B-BUT THEY STING, RIGHT?
Run!

ARE ANY OF YOU ALLERGIC?
THEN YOU HAVE NOTHING TO WORRY ABOUT. HONEYBEES ARE GENTLE.

THIS ONE'S LIKELY A WORKER BEE, AS THE ONES YOU SEE OUTSIDE THE HIVE TYPICALLY ARE.
THEY GATHER POLLEN AND BRING IT BACK HOME TO MAKE HONEY.

AND THEY WANT TO STING YOU JUST AS MUCH AS YOU WANT TO BE STUNG.

HOW DO YOU KNOW SO MUCH ABOUT BEES?
OUR FATHER TOOK US TO A BEE FARM LAST SUMMER.
IT WAS PRETTY COOL.
WE GOT TO PUT ON THOSE WEIRD SUITS AND LOOK AT THE COMBS.

I'VE NEVER SEEN A HIVE BEFORE.
IT LOOKS LIKE THEY'RE ALL...CROWDED TOGETHER.
THEY'RE USUALLY INSIDE TREE HOLLOWS.

AND CROWDED, YES. BUT PURPOSELY SO.
THOUGH THE HONEYBEES YOU SEE OUTSIDE ARE USUALLY WORKERS, INSIDE THERE'S STRUCTURE. A SOCIETY, IF YOU WILL.

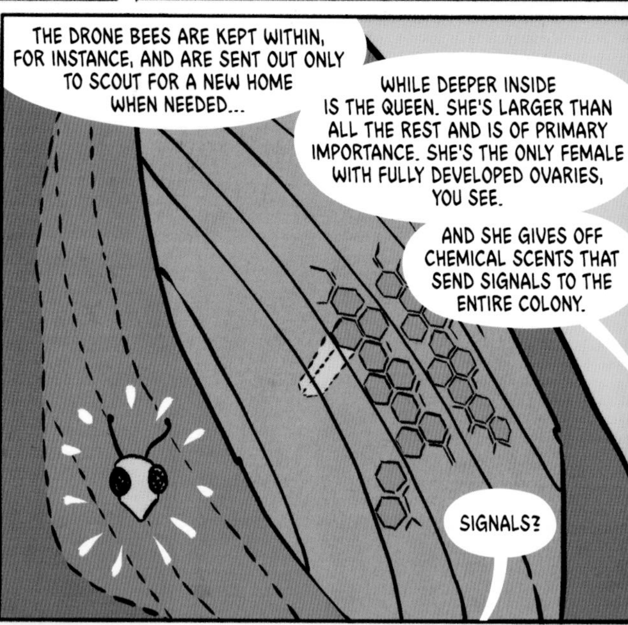
THE DRONE BEES ARE KEPT WITHIN, FOR INSTANCE, AND ARE SENT OUT ONLY TO SCOUT FOR A NEW HOME WHEN NEEDED...
WHILE DEEPER INSIDE IS THE QUEEN. SHE'S LARGER THAN ALL THE REST AND IS OF PRIMARY IMPORTANCE. SHE'S THE ONLY FEMALE WITH FULLY DEVELOPED OVARIES, YOU SEE.
AND SHE GIVES OFF CHEMICAL SCENTS THAT SEND SIGNALS TO THE ENTIRE COLONY.
SIGNALS?

INDEED. SIGNALS THAT INSTRUCT THE HIVE WHAT TO DO.
SO, EVERYTHING THE BEES DO...THEY DO FOR THE QUEEN?
YES AND NO.

THE QUEEN YOU MIGHT IMAGINE AS THE MIND OF THE HIVE, WHILE ALL THE OTHERS ACT ON THAT MIND'S BEHALF.
BUT THE HIVE IS STILL A COLLECTIVE. NONE WOULD EXIST WITHOUT ALL.

AND IF SOMETHING CHANGES, IF THE QUEEN DIES, FOR INSTANCE, THEN ANOTHER QUEEN IS CHOSEN, AND THE PROCESS REPEATS ITSELF.

I'M NOT WORRIED ABOUT PLAYING HERE.

YEAH, ME NEITHER.
BZZ

GOOD! THEN LET'S RESUME. WE HAVE MERE HOURS BEFORE DINNER.

BZZ
Crooked...

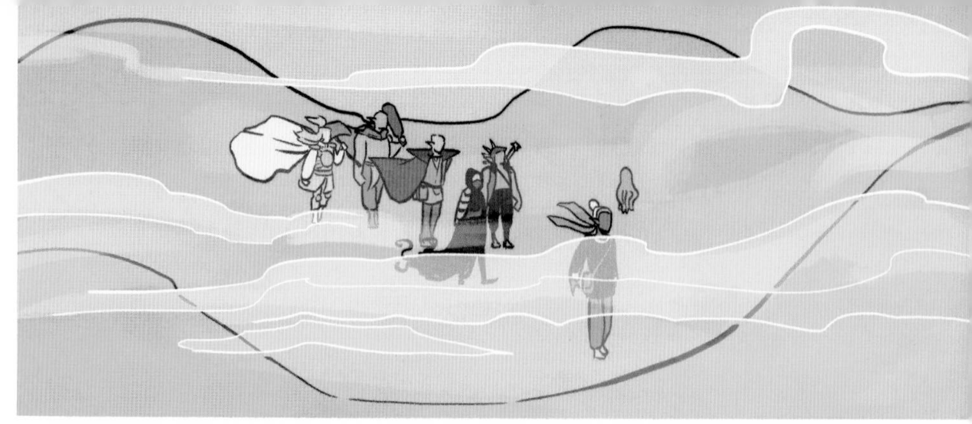

I CAN BARELY SEE!
AH, DUDES, THIS STORM'S KILLING MY LUTE!

IT'S ONLY GETTING WORSE. WE NEED TO DO SOMETHING.
I HAVE AN IDEA.

SAPARTHACAL'JIKI NAMAGI!

SER BRIDGER! GRUNTUS! USE YOUR WEAPONS AS POLES!

WELL DONE, EVERYONE.
WHA!

IT--IT STARTED JUMPING AROUND!
JUMPING AROUND?
YEAH! LIKE, VIBRATING!

IT WAS JUST SITTING IN THAT TOMB-- AFTER WE DEFEATED THE FOG OF FORGETFULNESS.
IT HAS TO BE IMPORTANT.
MAY I?

MARASTIAL' JIBAKI'TALOO...

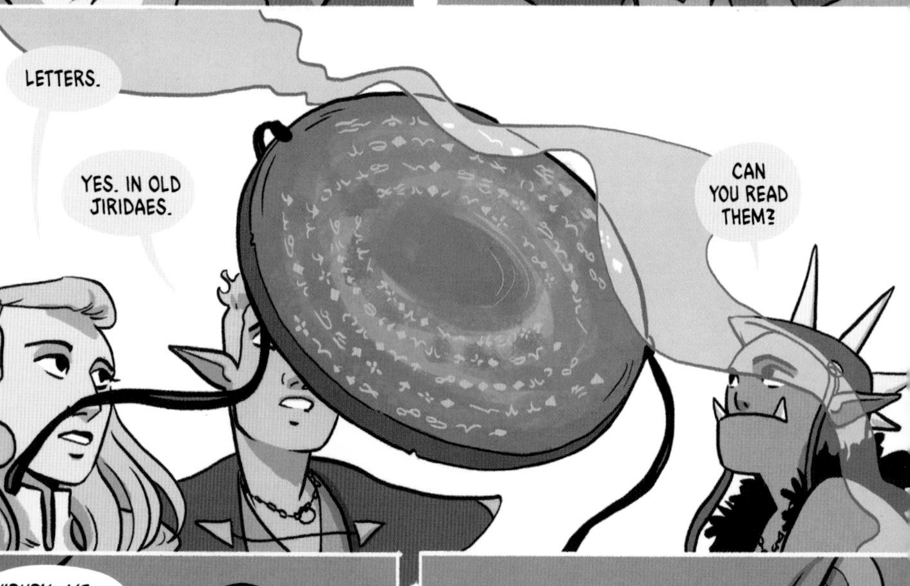
LETTERS.
YES. IN OLD JIRIDAES.
CAN YOU READ THEM?

"BURY...ME... IN THE OCEAN... OF GLASS.
"GROW ME...WITH WATER...FIRE...AND ASH.
"FROM THERE...MY LIGHT...WILL CLEAR THE WAY.
"TO THE GREAT...SEEKER'S TOWER...WITH THE MOON IN HALF SWAY."

AN OCEAN OF GLASS.

GRUNT?
GLASS IS MADE OF SAND.
HERE'S SOME WATER!

SOME FIRE.

...
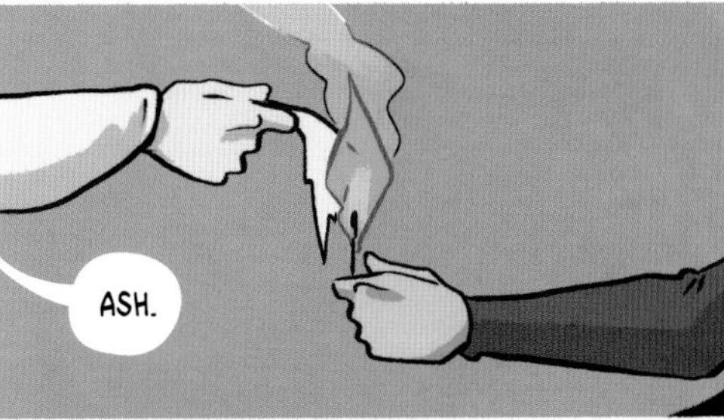
ASH.

MMMMMMMMMMMM

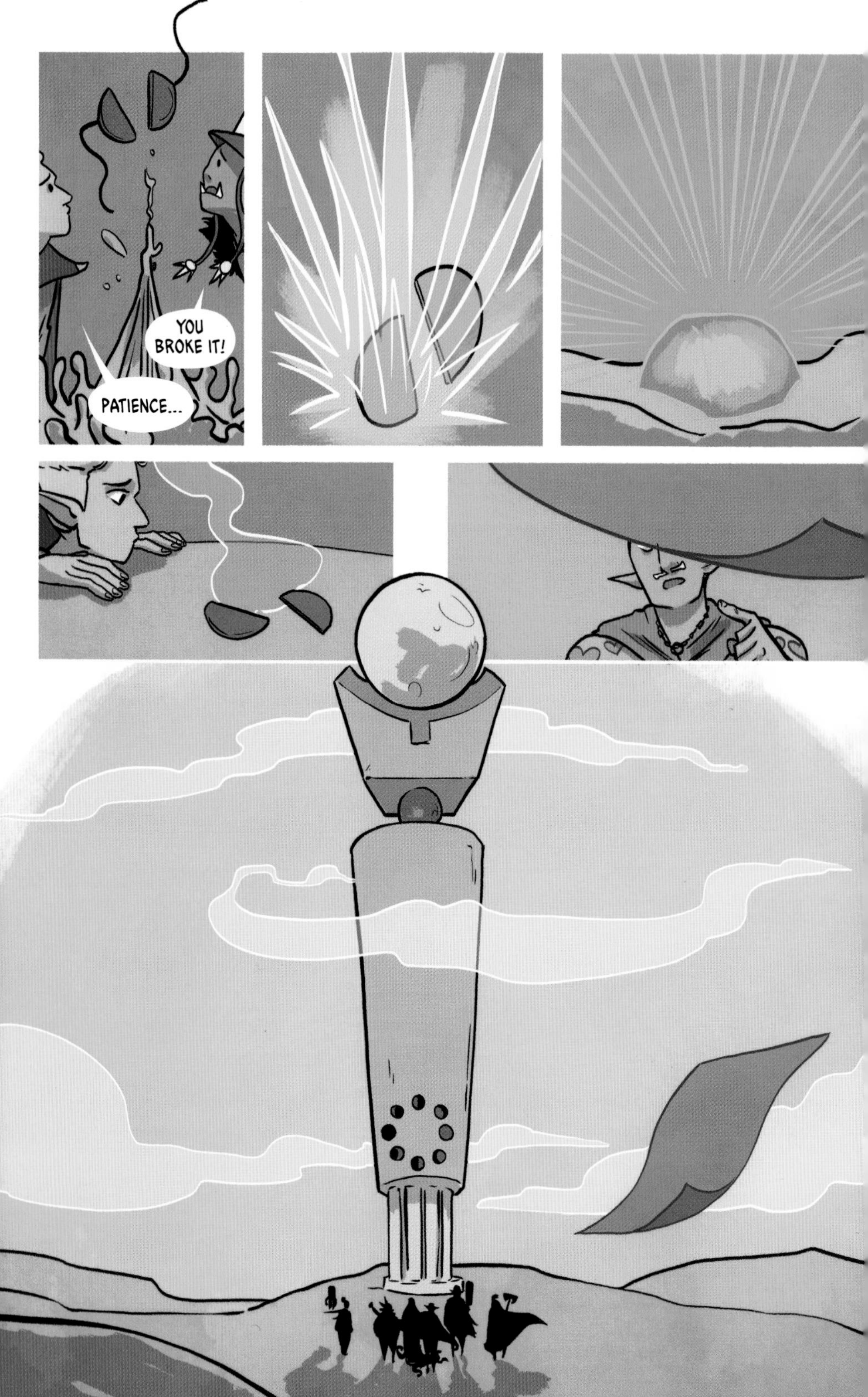
YOU BROKE IT!
PATIENCE...

VOLIN, DUDE! THAT WAS AMAZING!
INDEED. QUITE IMPRESSIVE, YES.
GRUUUUUNT!

AN IMPRESSIVE DISPLAY, MASTER VOLIN. NOT THAT I'M SURPRISED IN THE LEAST.

MASTER VOLIN, HE'S ♪ HAD OUR HEARTS STOLEN!
BRINGING THE ♫ KNOWLEDGE WHEN WE NEED IT LIKE ♪ HE'S GOLDEN!
GOLDEN! GOLDEN ♫ VOLIN!

COME ON, MOG... WHOEVER YOU ARE!
...
ALAS, I CANNOT JOIN YOU.

WHY NOT?
THE MAGIC THAT ALLOWED ME TO SEARCH THIS WORLD FOR CHAMPIONS LIKE YOURSELVES ALSO LIMITS ME FROM RETURNING HOME.

THAT IS... CRUEL.
WHEN YOU UNDERSTAND THE WAYS OF GREENMOON--
YOU UNDERSTAND THAT ALL MAGIC IS GIVE AND TAKE.

NOW GO. BE SWIFT. AND BRING THE TOWER OF GREENMOON BACK TO OUR LANDS SO THAT I MAY ONE DAY SEE IT AGAIN WITH MY OWN EYES.
WHO WANTS TO GO IN FIRST?

LET'S ALL GO IN... TOGETHER.

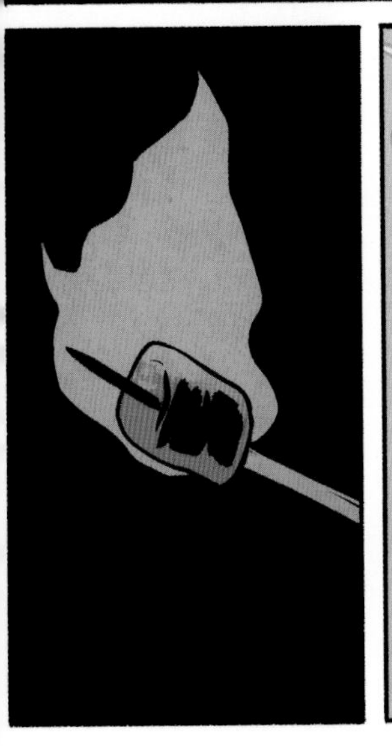

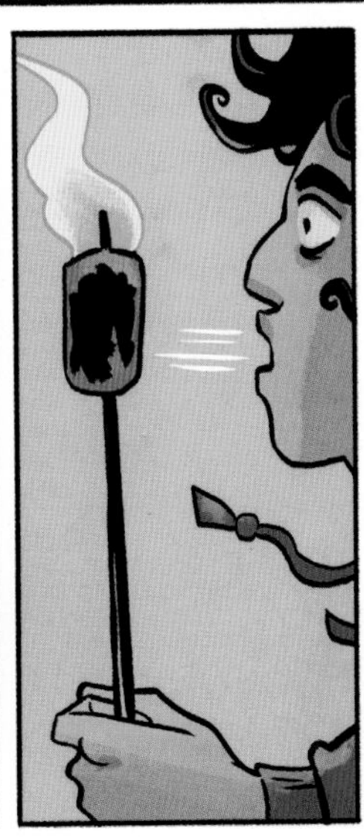

QUICK, PUT IT ON THE CHOCOLATE.

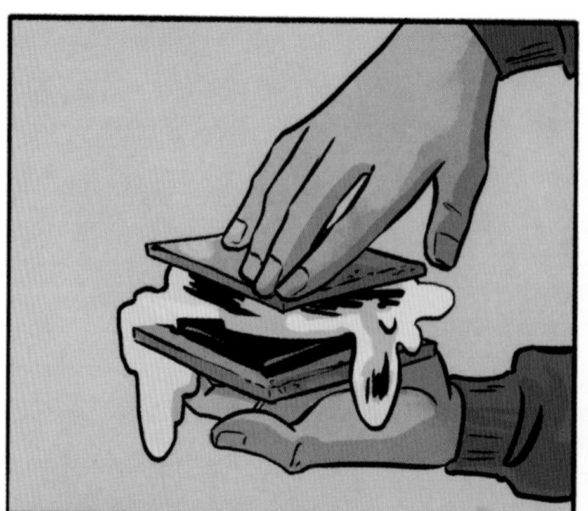

PFF. STILL GONNA EAT IT.

WANT ANOTHER ONE?

BZZZ

OK, EVERYONE READY?

THREE, TWO, ONE...
FLASHLIGHTS OFF!

WANT TO STAR SEARCH?
STAR SEARCH?
CONSTELLATIONS.

LIBRA! THAT'S LIBRA!
YOU'RE RIGHT. WOW...IT'S BEAUTIFUL.
I SEE IT!
WHERE?

RIGHT THERE. TWO SCALES.
OH...

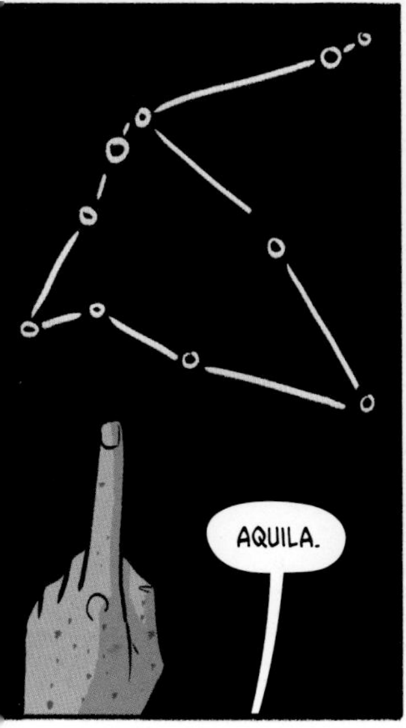
AQUILA.

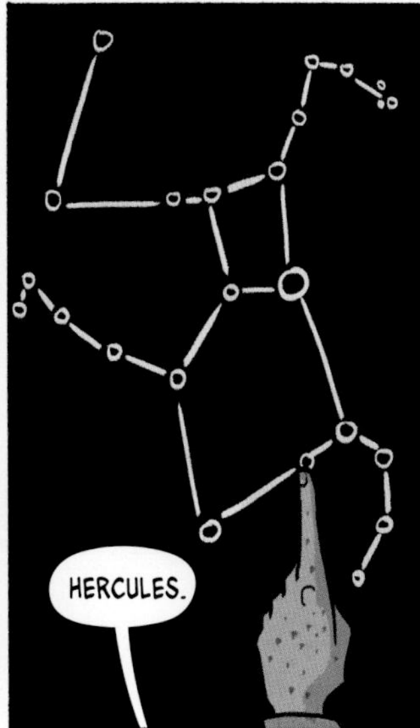
HERCULES.

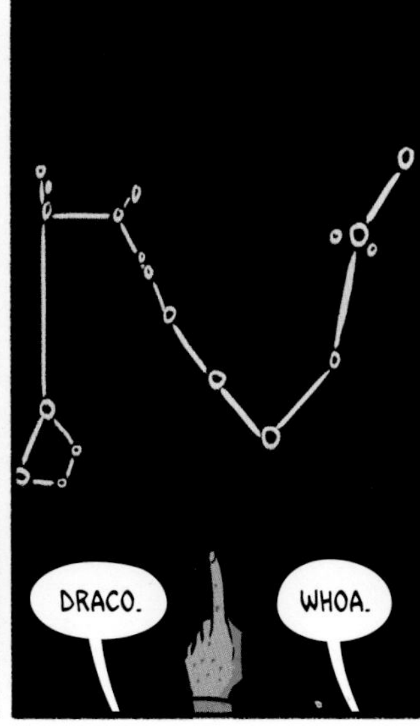
DRACO.
WHOA.

YOU KNOW SO MUCH ABOUT STARS.
OH, WELL, NOT REALLY. WE JUST GO CAMPING A LOT. AND MY UNCLE...EVER SINCE I WAS LITTLE, HE'S SENT ME ALL THESE BOOKS ABOUT ASTRONOMY...
YOU KNOW THE KIND I MEAN?

NO. NOT REALLY.
...
WHEN DID YOU START DRAWING?

Sick.
I...I DON'T KNOW. CAN'T REMEMBER.
NO, WAIT. THAT'S RIGHT. MY MOM SAID SHE KNEW I LIKED DRAWING BECAUSE I WOULD DRAW ON EVERYTHING, EVEN THINGS I SHOULDN'T. LIKE WALLS.
HA HA.
I THINK SHE HATED IT.

I...KNOW I'M WEIRD SOMETIMES.
IT'S BECAUSE OF THE WAY I THINK.
IT'S HARD FOR ME TO TALK ABOUT, BUT MY THOUGHTS GET JUMBLED SOMETIMES.
THOUGHTS JUST...FORCE THEIR WAY THROUGH. THOUGHTS I DON'T WANT.

ISAAC...I LIKE THAT YOU'RE WEIRD.
I'M ACTUALLY WEIRD, TOO. DID YOU KNOW THAT?
NO.

IT'S TRUE. I THINK IT STARTED A FEW YEARS AGO.
I STARTED TO SEE MYSELF AS DIFFERENT FROM SOME PEOPLE, AND I DIDN'T KNOW WHAT THAT MEANT.
HOW?

WELL...I GUESS THAT SOMETIMES I FELT LIKE I WAS A BOY. OTHER TIMES, A GIRL. AND THEN, NOT REALLY A BOY *OR* A GIRL...

I STARTED TO THINK THAT I WAS SOMEWHERE BETWEEN THE TWO OR BOTH AT THE SAME TIME.
AND THAT FELT WEIRD. BECAUSE MANY OTHERS SEEMED SO...SET THAT WAY. SO ONE-SIDED. IT WAS DIFFICULT TO UNDERSTAND.

...THAT SOUNDS... HARD.
KINDA, YEAH... BUT THEN, I STARTED TO SEE THAT ALL THOSE OTHER PEOPLE? THE ONES WHO SEEM SO ONE-SIDED? SO SET?
THEY'RE ACTUALLY AS WEIRD AS I AM. JUST IN DIFFERENT WAYS.
AND FOR SO MANY DIFFERENT REASONS...

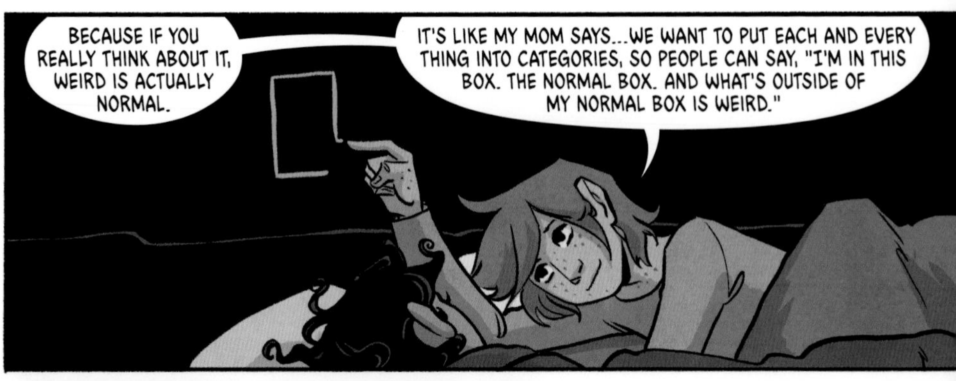
BECAUSE IF YOU REALLY THINK ABOUT IT, WEIRD IS ACTUALLY NORMAL.
IT'S LIKE MY MOM SAYS...WE WANT TO PUT EACH AND EVERY THING INTO CATEGORIES, SO PEOPLE CAN SAY, "I'M IN THIS BOX. THE NORMAL BOX. AND WHAT'S OUTSIDE OF MY NORMAL BOX IS WEIRD."

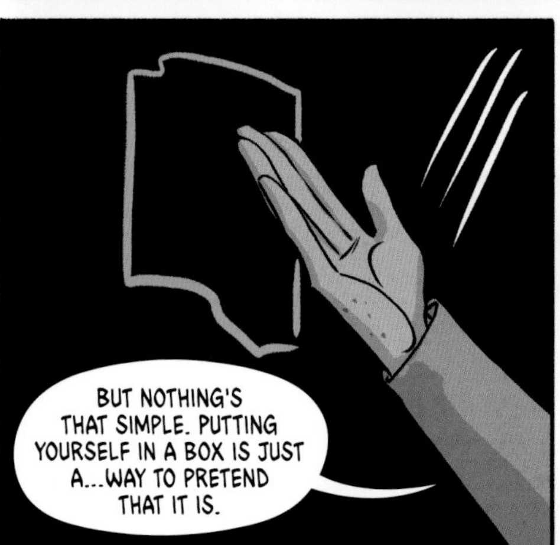
BUT NOTHING'S THAT SIMPLE. PUTTING YOURSELF IN A BOX IS JUST A...WAY TO PRETEND THAT IT IS.

I THINK WHAT I'M SAYING IS THAT PEOPLE LIKE US, WHO KNOW WE'RE WEIRD? WE NEED TO STICK TOGETHER. SO THAT SOMEDAY...WE CHANGE WHAT NORMAL MEANS.

I SAW A METEOR!
I AS WELL! OR PERHAPS IT WAS AN ALIEN CRAFT. A SAUCER, IN COMMON PARLANCE.
AW MAN, DON'T TALK ABOUT ALIENS OUT HERE!
HA
HA
HA
HA

BZZ

HEY, MOM. DID YOU STILL WANT TO GO TO RILEY'S TODAY?
...HUH?
RILEY'S. FOR YARN.
WWWWWW-

...
tak
tak
tak

ISAAC, DARLING.
OH, YEAH?
WHO ARE YOU CHATTING WITH?

MICAH.
I SEE.
MICAH.

I'M GLAD YOU HAVE NEW FRIENDS, DARLING. BUT I DON'T WANT YOU TO GET CARRIED AWAY.
...

ISAAC!
HUH?

YOU'VE BEEN IGNORING ME LATELY. ALL THE TIME. MAYBE YOU DON'T SEE IT, BUT I DO.
AND IT'S NOT JUST THAT... YOU'VE BEEN EXHIBITING BEHAVIOR LATELY THAT WORRIES ME.
IT'S LIKE YOU'RE LIVING IN OUR OWN UNIVERSE. AND IT'S HAVING REAL REPERCUSSIONS.
LIKE WHAT?

WELL, LIKE YOUR TEST, FOR ONE.
I RETOOK IT!
AND YOU GOT A B-MINUS! BARELY A STEP UP FROM WHERE YOU WERE BEFORE.

I TRIED MY HARDEST. I DID WHAT I COULD.
YOU DIDN'T TRY YOUR HARDEST, BECAUSE YOU'VE BEEN DISTRACTED.
DISTRACTED BY YOUR NEW FRIENDS. IT'S LIKE DR. PENNY SAID.

MAINTAINING FOCUS AND MINIMIZING OUTSIDE STRESSORS ARE GOING TO BE THE KEY...

...TO MANAGING YOUR CONDITION.
I'M NOT STRESSED!
BZZZ
YOU'RE COMPLETELY UNFOCUSED. YOU'RE WANDERING. AND IT'S GOING TO ***HURT*** YOU.

YOU THINK I'M SO S-SICK! AND MAYBE I AM, BUT I'M ALSO A LOT OF THINGS. A LOT OF THINGS YOU DON'T UNDERSTAND!
I WISH YOU'D JUST LEAVE ME ALONE!

ISAAC...
YOU'RE FINISHED WITH THAT GAME.
BUT!
I SAID ***FINISHED!***

WE'VE HAD A DIFFICULT YEAR. YOUR DAD. YOUR DIAGNOSIS. A NEW SCHOOL.
WE NEED TO PULL THINGS BACK. SPEND TIME TOGETHER. UNDERSTAND WHAT IT IS YOU'RE GOING TO NEED TO FACE YOUR TROUBLES GOING FORWARD.

MOM...I LOVE PLAYING. AND IT'S NOT BAD. NOT BAD AT ALL. I SWEAR. IT'S--
YOU'RE FINISHED WITH THE GAME, ISAAC. THIS CONVERSATION IS OVER.

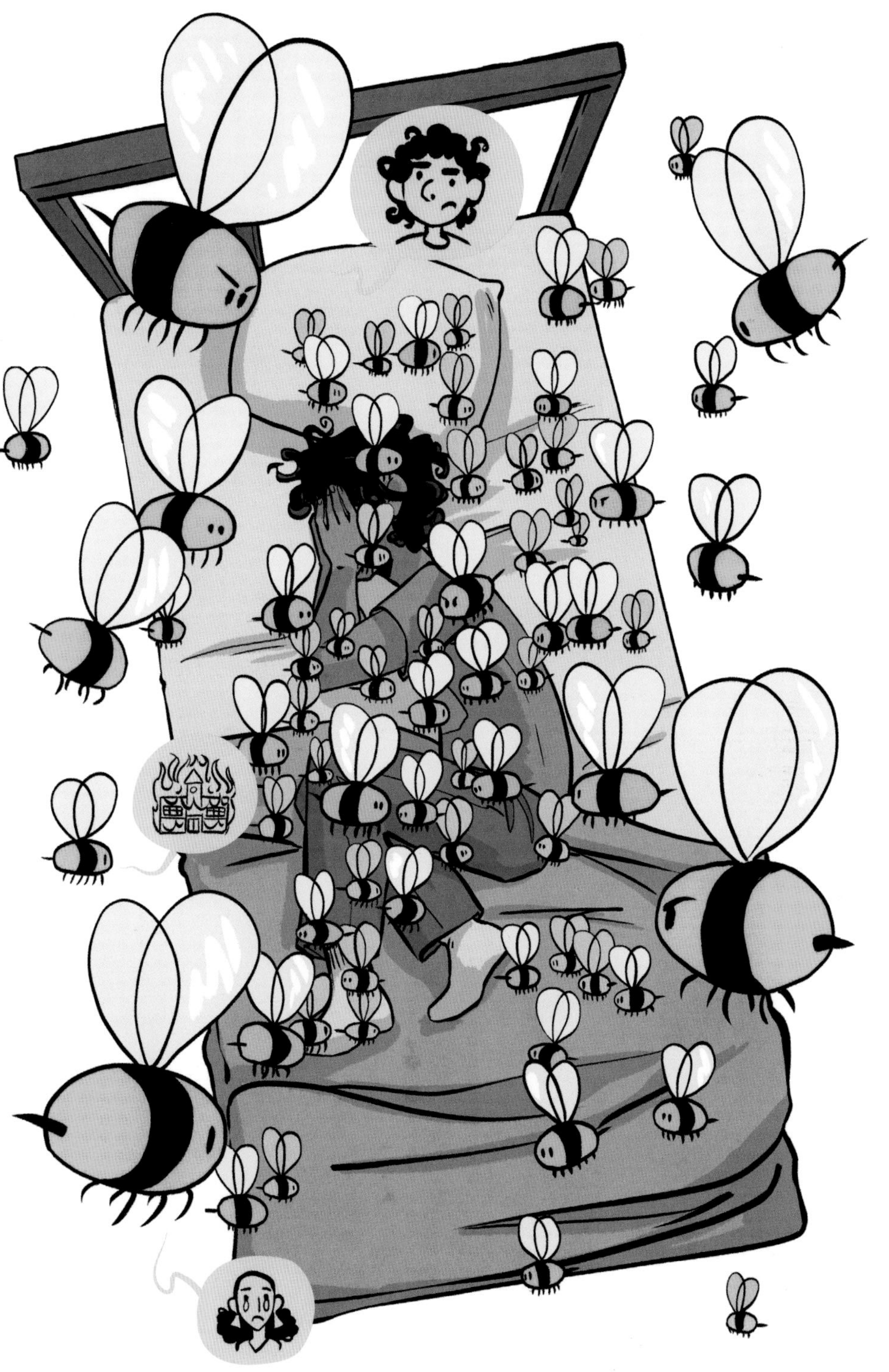

BZZ

BZZ

BZZ

Are you okay?
BZZ

ZZZZ

Can we just talk?
I miss you. :(<3

Told you you're sick.
Better this way-- tug your ear.

You're uglier than ever.
Diseased and ugly and horrible.
You'll be alone forever.
You cause pain.
Shouldn't exist.

Cut uneven.
Tug your ear five times to correct.
ISAAC, DARLING.
Six times.

HOW WAS YOUR TUTORING SESSION THIS MORNING?
OH...
Tug your ear!
IT WAS GOOD.

OH, I'M SO GLAD. TED WAS A RECOMMENDATION FROM MY FRIEND LARISSA AT WORK.
HER DAUGHTER HAS SOME...SPECIAL NEEDS. SO I THOUGHT HE MIGHT BE GOOD FOR YOU AS WELL.
BEEDILOOP BEEDILOOP
OH!

SORRY, DARLING--HELLO? YES, SPEAKING. OH, HI, GERALD. NO. THAT WON'T BE NECESSARY. ONLY IF HE'S WILLING TO SIGN...

HEY.
ISAAC?

I WANTED TO TELL YOU SOMETHING...
Tug your ear.
Three more times.

THERE'S THIS STORE I SAW THE OTHER DAY. I THINK IT'S CALLED LEVEL UP.
AND THEY HAD THIS SIGN ON THE DOOR...SOMETHING ABOUT THEM HOSTING, LIKE, WEEKLY SWAMPS & SORCERY GAMES, I THINK.

...OK.
I JUST... LOOK, IT'S NEAR THE LIBRARY, OK? AND I JUST THOUGHT...

IT DOESN'T MATTER. MOM WON'T LET ME.
YEAH, I KNOW. BUT...
WELL, THAT'S RIDICULOUS...
I CAN MAKE SURE SHE DOESN'T FIND OUT.
If you go, then she'll

BUT...WHY?
WHY WHAT?
WHY WOULD YOU...DO THAT? DON'T YOU... HATE ME?
I JUST--I JUST WILL, OK?

...YOUR BIGGEST HURDLE WILL BE LEARNING TO TRUST YOURSELF.
FUEL
Sick.
Disgusting.
They all hate you.

MIRIAM?
...THANKS.
OK, GERALD. BYE-BYE, NOW.

NOW. WHERE WERE WE?

LEVELUP!

OPEN RPGS
TUES + THURS
2 PM!

OPEN

MIRIAM... WHY ARE YOU DOING THIS?
YEAH. I'M SURE.
YOU SURE?

I JUST THINK...YOU COULD USE A BIG SISTER. AND I COULD USE A LITTLE BROTHER.
WE CAN DEPEND ON EACH OTHER A LITTLE MORE, YOU KNOW?

2PM!

BRRRRNG

ANYTHING I CAN HELP YOU WITH?
OH, UH...
I SAW THAT YOU HAVE, UM, OPEN GAMES? RPGS? HERE?

SURE DO. IN FACT, ONE OF THEM'S ABOUT TO START RIGHT NOW.
WANT TO SEE IF YOU CAN JOIN UP?
LARPing's
t a Hobby,
It's a
LIFESTYLE
EMPLO
ONLY
UH... OK.
BZZ

HEY, FOLKS. ANY ROOM FOR ONE MORE?
ARPing's

I'M ISAAC...I HAVE A CHARACTER THAT I MADE FOR SWAMPS & SORCERY?
...
WHAT EDITION DO YOU PLAY?

THIRD.
PFF. THIRD IS VASTLY INFERIOR TO FOURTH. YOU PROBABLY DON'T EVEN KNOW ABOUT ADVANCED GRID COMBAT.
RELAX, WALTER. IT'S NOT LIKE YOU DID EITHER BEFORE LAST MONTH.

I'M TRYING TO PROTECT THE INTEGRITY OF THE GAME!

OF COURSE YOU CAN JOIN. YOUR NAME IS ISAAC?
I'M LEE... SHE/HER.

AND THIS IS LISA, SHE/HER.
OUR GM, WALTER, HE/HIM.
FRED, THEY/THEM.
MOHAN, HE/HIM.
HEY.

WELCOME TO THE FOLD, ISAAC.
NOW, WHERE WERE WE, WALTER?
...

YOU'RE PART OF A CONVOY GUARDING A WAGON TRAIN. EACH OF YOU PICKED UP THE JOB FROM A MERCENARY OFFICE NEAR BORGAR'S KEEP.
AS FOR WHAT'S IN THE CONVOY, YOU HAVE NO IDEA...

CHILDREN! HOW WAS YOUR TIME AT THE LIBRARY?
GOOD, MOM.

IT JUST DELIGHTS ME, SEEING THE TWO OF YOU SPEND TIME TOGETHER.
AND, ISAAC, DARLING, TELL ME, WERE YOU ABLE TO FOCUS BETTER AT THE LIBRARY?
Liar.
OH, UH, YEAH, A LOT BETTER.
Your fault

I KNEW IT. YOU NEED A CONTROLLED ENVIRONMENT TO REALLY CONCENTRATE. IT'S WONDERFUL TO THINK ABOUT HOW MUCH THIS WILL HELP YOU IN THE FUTURE.
What future?
YEAH...

DINNER IN THIRTY MINUTES!

Tug your ear five times.
ZIPPP

wamps & Sorcery
me Master's Atlas
Tug your ear fi--

Swamps & Sorcery
Game Master's Atlas
BZZ

CLICK

KING
SUPERMARKET

YOU TWO CAN TAKE CARE OF PRODUCE.
AND WE CAN MEET AT THE REGISTER IN TWENTY MINUTES. OK?
Tug your ear.
OK.

Two more times...
B-DING
WHO'S THAT?

NO ONE!
I DIDN'T MEAN TO... SORRY.

NO, NO...IT'S OK. HIS NAME'S JOSH. JOSH LEWIS.
COOL. A FRIEND AT SCHOOL?
YEAH. WELL, NO. WELL...

PROMISE NOT TO TELL ANYONE?
Three more times.
YEAH, DEFINITELY.
I THINK HE'S MY BOYFRIEND NOW.

WHOOOOOA... BOYFRIEND.
SHH.
THAT'S AWESOME! UH, CONGRATS?

HA HA HA HA

THANKS, LITTLE BROTHER. JUST DON'T TELL MOM, OK? NOT THAT SHE'D CARE.
...

I THINK SHE DOES.
Selfish. Your fault.
DOES WHAT?
CARE. IT'S JUST...SHE DOESN'T KNOW HOW TO SEE US, I THINK.
IT'S LIKE SHE'S STUCK ON WHO WE WERE WHEN WE WERE LITTLE.

...OR SHE'S STUCK ON WHO SHE THINKS WE SHOULD BE.
EEP!

ISAAC?

THAT'S A GOOD IDEA.
YOU THINK IT'LL WORK?

WHAT HAVE WE TO LOSE?
TRYING SUGGESTS A POSSIBILITY OF SUCCESS, AT THE VERY LEAST.
TRUE...

Idiot. So stupid.
They always hated you.
Pull your ear five times.

Bad person.
HEY... THEY'RE GONE NOW.
Horrible.

Dirty. Filthy.
THANKS.

HEY, ISAAC?
YEAH?

YOU WANNA GRAB THE APPLES?
OK.

LEVEL UP!

THREE.
THREE PLUS THIRTEEN UNHOLY FIRE DAMAGE.
SAME GOES FOR ALL OF YOU.

COME ON, WALTER! THAT'LL KILL OFF THREE OF US!
WELL, YOU SHOULDN'T HAVE BEEN SO RECKLESS IN YOUR DECISION-MAKING.

IT FEELS LIKE YOU'VE BEEN TRYING TO SABOTAGE US.
YEAH. THIS HAS OFFICIALLY STOPPED BEING FUN.

FINE!
SWAPP
YOU DON'T LIKE THE WAY I GAME, I'LL TAKE MY SKILLS ELSEWHERE!

WELL. I GUESS THAT'S THAT.
YEAH. WE SHOULD HAVE FOUND SOMEONE ELSE. WALTER'S KIND OF A JERK.

SO...YOU GUYS ARE JUST LEAVING?
WHAT ELSE ARE WE SUPPOSED TO DO?
YEAH, MAN. I LIKE TO PLAY, BUT I'M NOT A GM.
YOU WANT TO MEET UP NEXT WEEK FOR SOME ENCHANTMENT?
OH... I'VE BEEN WANTING TO TRY MY NEW DECK.

YOU CAN JOIN US IF YOU WANT, IZZY. OK IF I CALL YOU IZZY?
OH...YEAH, OK. AND THANKS.

LATER, IZZY!
CAN I CATCH A RIDE WITH YOU?
OH, ME TOO?
SURE.

Your fault. Always your fault.
Tug your ear five times.
Sick.

YOU KNOW, I WAS THINKING...

...WHAT IF WE GO ON A SHORT VACATION LATER THIS SUMMER?
YOUR GRANDPARENTS ARE GOING TO BE RENTING A CABIN NEAR LOVELAND.
IT COULD BE NICE TO GET AWAY FOR A DAY OR TWO. DON'T YOU THINK?

WELL, THAT SOUNDS--
BING BONG

WAIT! MIRIAM? WHO WOULD BE COMING AROUND THIS LATE?
BUT...
IT'S OK, MOM.

COME IN!
UH... UH...

SHOES OFF, PLEASE.
WHY, HELLO... A LITTLE LATE, DON'T YOU THINK? I WASN'T EXPECTING...UM...

GREETINGS, ESTEEMED MRS. ITKIN. I AM CALLED CARMEN, FIRST OF HER NAME.
I'M JAIME. WHAT SHE SAID. BUT WITH LESS WORDS.

...WE JUST WANTED TO BRING SOMETHING OVER FOR ISAAC.
A PRESENT!
YEP.

A PRESENT? I SEE. I...ARE YOU HUNGRY? THIRSTY? IT'S A LITTLE LATE FOR IT, BUT I HAVE LEMONADE.
AH, MY PREFERRED BEVERAGE. I WOULD LIKE A SERVING, THANK YOU. AND MIGHT YOU HARBOR ICE?

...

AHEM. VOLIN OF THE HALL OF MURMURS.
WE HAVE PROCURED THIS CHEST FROM THE SANDS OF KURADAI--
AND ARE PRESENTING IT TO YOU ON BEHALF OF THE GREENMOON GUILD. ITS TREASURES ARE MEANT FOR YOU AND YOU ALONE.

BUT ALSO, YOU CAN TOTALLY OPEN IT NOW.
OH.

1
2
3
4

I DON'T KNOW WHAT TO...
THANK YOU...

DID YOUR DAD MAKE THESE?
YEP! WELL, KINDA. WE HELPED.
YES, WE PARTICIPATED IN THE CONFECTIONING.
I ADDED SPRINKLES.

WOULD YOU LIKE ONE, MRS. ITKIN?
OH, I DON'T KNOW IF I SHOULD...
THEY'RE REALLY GOOD!
...I *ACCIDENTALLY* ATE ONE ALREADY.

MMM!

THIS IS VERY, VERY GOOD.
I'M GLAD YOU LIKE IT.
THESE DICE ARE AMAZING...
WE THOUGHT THEY MATCHED VOLIN'S CLOTHING.

WHAT HAVE YOU BEEN UP TO, MY DUDE?
OH, JUST STUDYING... I HAVE A TUTOR.
YEAH, MY PARENTS GOT ONE FOR ME, TOO.
REALLY?

THEY'RE TRYING TO PREP ME FOR NEXT YEAR. IT'S KIND OF ABSURD.
HMPH. "ABSURD," INDEED.
I'D PERSONALLY PREFER A PRIVATE TUTOR TO PREPARE ME FOR STANDARDIZED TESTING.
AND AGAIN, ANOTHER DIFFERENCE BETWEEN ME AND MY TWIN SISTER.

HOW DID YOU ALL GET HERE TONIGHT, ANYHOW?
OUR FATHER PROVIDED PORTAGE. HE NOW AWAITS US OUTSIDE.
OH! SHOULD WE INVITE HIM IN?

IT'S OK, MRS. ITKIN. WE JUST WANTED TO STOP BY AND SAY HELLO.
WE JUST... WE REALLY CARE ABOUT ISAAC.

HE HAS A DIGNIFIED PERSONALITY.
AND HE'S A SUPER-SICK ARTIST.
AND HE'S ALWAYS NICE.
FUNNY, TOO.

MOST OF ALL, I--I MEAN *WE*, MISS HIM.

...I APPRECIATE YOUR CONCERN, CHILDREN. I REALLY DO. BUT ISAAC HAS HAD A DIFFICULT YEAR. AND HE IS DOING WELL--HERE AT HOME.
I KNOW THAT'S HARD FOR YOU ALL TO UNDERSTAND. BUT IT'S THE RIGHT THING.

...THANK YOU, MRS. ITKIN.

WELL. THAT WAS ODD. AND INAPPROPRIATE, PERHAPS.
I THINK IT WAS NICE.

LOTS OF THINGS ARE NICE, MIRIAM. IT DOESN'T MEAN THEY'RE HELPFUL.
MOM...
LOOK...

IN WHAT UNIVERSE IS THIS ***NOT*** GOOD FOR ISAAC?
...

THEY REALLY ARE NICE KIDS, AREN'T THEY?
YES, MOM. THEY ARE. AND ISAAC...HE IS, TOO.
I KNOW THAT, MIRIAM.

I KNOW YOU DO...BUT HE ALSO NEEDS TO BE ALLOWED TO BE AROUND OTHER PEOPLE LIKE HIM.
I'M NOT HIDING HIM. I'M KEEPING HIM SAFE.
HE IS SAFE, MOM. WITH HIS FRIENDS.
YOU CAN'T... YOU CAN'T DECIDE HOW HE FEELS.

HOW DO YOU KNOW WHAT'S BEST FOR HIM?
WHERE HAVE YOU BEEN, THROUGH ALL HIS APPOINTMENTS?
WITH YOUR FATHER DOING WHATEVER HE'S DOING NOW, IT ALL FALLS ON ME, MIRIAM. ME.

WHERE HAVE I BEEN, MOM? I'VE BEEN RIGHT HERE. THE WHOLE TIME!
THE PROBLEM HERE IS THAT YOU CAN'T SEE ME.

LevelUP!
OPEN RPGS
TUES + THURS
2 PM!

OH, HEY, IZZY. GLAD YOU SHOWED.
HEY HEY.
OH, HI.
Stupid. Sound stupid.

WANT TO JOIN THE NEXT GAME?
I DON'T HAVE A DECK FOR ENCHANTMENT. I ACTUALLY, UM, WAS HOPING WALTER OR SOMEONE CAME BACK. TO GM.

NAH, HE'S STILL SULKING.
KIND OF RIDICULOUS, IF YOU ASK ME. I SPENT SO MUCH TIME ON MY CHARACTER.
HEY, IZZY--WHAT ABOUT YOU?

HUH?
YEAH, WHY DON'T YOU GM? DIDN'T YOU SAY YOU READ THE S&S ATLAS?
YEAH, BUT...
Tug your ear.
If you don't tug your ear, they'll hate you.

I ONLY JUST FINISHED READING IT A COUPLE WEEKS AGO.
THAT'S MORE THAN ANY OF US HAVE DONE.

WHAT DO YOU THINK, IZZY? WANNA GIVE IT A GO?
BZZ

SEE YOU ALL NEXT WEEK!
BYE, IZZY!

MR. BODUM?
BZZ
ISAAC!

I SHOULDN'T BE SURPRISED THAT I'D RUN INTO YOU HERE.
HA HA...HAVE YOU BEEN HERE BEFORE?

THIS IS ACTUALLY MY FIRST TIME! ALL THAT TALKING ABOUT ROLE-PLAYING GAMES WITH YOU PIQUED MY INTEREST.
AND I ASSUME FROM SEEING YOU HERE THAT YOU'RE STILL PLAYING SWAMPS & SORCERY?
WELL, KINDA...

THAT'S...MY GROUP. AND IT, WELL...IT LOOKS LIKE I'M GOING TO BE GM FOR THE FIRST TIME?
THAT'S WONDERFUL, ISAAC!

YEAH, I, UH...I THINK SO! A LITTLE NERVOUS...
THESE ARE THE FRIENDS YOU WERE PLAYING WITH PREVIOUSLY?

UH, NO. NOT THEM. I...MY MOM TOLD ME I HAD TO STOP PLAYING.
SHE FINALLY WENT AHEAD AND RESTRICTED YOU, HUH?
YEAH...

BUT SHE'S STILL LETTING YOU COME HERE TO PLAY?
HEH...NOT EXACTLY?
MY SISTER AND I ARE SUPPOSED TO BE STUDYING AT THE LIBRARY.
I COME HERE INSTEAD. AND UH...MY SISTER DOESN'T TELL OUR MOM.

B-BUT IT DOESN'T INTERFERE WITH MY SUMMER TUTORING, I PROMISE!
HA
HA
HA
HA

WELL, AS I SAID BEFORE, YOUR SECRET IS SAFE WITH ME.
I JUST HOPE YOU CAN RECONNECT WITH YOUR DEAR FRIENDS EVENTUALLY.
THEY SEEMED SO IMPORTANT TO YOU...IT'S A SHAME TO LET THAT FALL APART.

IF YOU CAN, TRY AND REMEMBER THAT SOMETIMES, WHEN OUR PARENTS SAY THEY'RE DOING SOMETHING FOR OUR SAKE--
THEY DON'T QUITE KNOW THEY'RE ACTUALLY DOING IT FOR THEMSELVES.
KEEP ON LEARNING TO TRUST YOURSELF. EVEN WHEN IT'S HARD.
THANKS, MR. BODUM. I'LL...I'LL TRY.

BY THE WAY, YOU MIGHT WANT TO CHECK OUT THIS ONE AS WELL, IF YOU WANT TO START A GAME.
AH, RIGHT. YES.

OPEN
I'LL BE PURCHASING THESE, PLEASE.
OK, THEN!
BYE, MR. BODUM!

SO THEN HE SAYS HE STILL TAKES BUBBLE BATHS!
BUT NO! THAT ACTUALLY SOUNDS LIKE FUN.

YEAH, IF YOU'RE FIVE?!
WELCOME BACK.

HEY, MOM.

DINNER IN THIRTY!
OK!

SEARCH FOR THE
STARFINDERS

SEARCH FOR THE
STARFINDERS

IS THAT RIGHT?
YES. HE'S BEEN IMPROVING MORE AND MORE OVER THE SUMMER. IT'S BEEN GREAT TO SEE.
I EXPECT HIS SCHOOLWORK WILL IMPROVE GREATLY WHEN THE QUARTER STARTS.

THANK YOU! HAVE A NICE DAY...

READY?
YEP!
BZZ

OOPS!
BZZ

BOOK SALE

OPEN

HEY, JUSTINE!
HEY, IZZY!

HEY, IZZY! I JUST MET YOUR FRIENDS.
INDEED! WE'VE BEEN MULLING OVER COOPERATIVE MECHANICS IN ENCHANTMENT, WHICH I DO THINK I'LL DABBLE IN WHEN THE OPPORTUNITY PRESENTS.

HEY.
HI.

I'M SORRY I DIDN'T TELL YOU... I JUST...
MY MOM...I HAD TO STOP PLAYING, AND I DIDN'T WANT TO.
SO I CAME HERE.
MIRIAM, SHE HELPED, AND--
ISAAC...
YOU DON'T NEED TO BE SORRY.
NO WAY, DUDE. WE UNDERSTAND. LIFE IS KINDA WEIRD SOMETIMES--THAT'S WHAT MY DAD SAYS.
YEAH. AND ANYWAY, THE REAL QUESTION IS...CAN WE JOIN?
YOU...YOU WANT TO PLAY?
UM, YEAH, DUDE!
FROM WHAT THESE FOLKS ARE SAYING, IT SOUNDS LIKE YOU GOT A PRETTY DANK QUEST GOING.
A PRIME OPPORTUNITY FOR BOBBERT'S JAM SKILLS TO SHINE...
BUT WHAT ABOUT GREENMOON? WE DIDN'T FINISH IT.

LAST I LOOKED, TIME AND SPACE WEREN'T COMING TO AN END TODAY. WE WILL FINISH OUR QUEST.
BUT IN THE MEANTIME, I'VE CREATED A HALF-LIZKIN MARAUDER WHO HAS A PENCHANT FOR ORCAVIAN HOT SAUCE.
HOT SAUCE

...THE ORDER OF GREENMOON.

AND NOW, WITH THE INTRODUCTIONS AT THEIR END, YOU TURN YOUR ATTENTION TO THE NEW LAND YOU'VE COME UPON. A PLACE WHERE PEOPLE HAVE FORGOTTEN HOW TO READ...

...AND STORIES TRAVEL OF A MYTHICAL FOUNTAIN THAT CAN RESTORE WHAT'S BEEN LOST.

RUBIX
ICE CREAM

SEE YA!
BYE!

BYE, EVERYONE!
BYE, MICAH.

HA HA HA
WHAT?

YOU TWO ARE TOO CUTE. IT MAKES ME HAPPY.
BZZ
WHAT DO YOU MEAN?
WHAT DO I MEAN?
YEAH.

HEY, EVEN IF YOU DON'T WANT TO TALK BOUT IT, IT DOESN'T MAKE YOU TWO ANY LESS ADORABLE.
HA HA...

SCHOOL STARTS BACK SOON ANYWAY, SO YOU'LL ALL BE ABLE TO SEE EACH OTHER WITHOUT HAVING TO HIDE FROM MOM.
OH YEAH, THAT'S RIGHT. SCHOOL.
Your fault.

MIRIAM?
YEAH?
I JUST WANTED TO SAY...THANK YOU.

OH, PLEASE, FOR WHAT?
FOR BEING...THERE. FOR ME.
BZZ

ANYTIME.

HI, MOM!
SORRY FOR BEING A LITTLE LATE, WE WERE--

MOM?
IN HERE!

SWAMPS + SORCERY RULEBOOK
SWAMPS + SORCERY
SWAMPS + SORCERY
SKETCHBOOK
LIMITLESS:

I WASN'T SURE WHICH ONES YOU ALREADY HAD...
SKETCHBOOK

BUT, MOM, I THOUGHT...
It's your fault. All of it.
I KNOW. I KNOW, DARLING.
HAVE A SEAT. BOTH OF YOU.

I BELIEVE I'VE BEEN... WRONG.
IN THINKING ABOUT MYSELF, WHAT *I* WANT, I HAVEN'T THOUGHT ENOUGH ABOUT WHAT YOU--
WHAT ***BOTH*** OF YOU--ACTUALLY NEED.

IT'S HARD FOR ME TO ADMIT...BUT I DON'T ALWAYS HAVE THE ANSWERS...
I NEED TO STOP PRETENDING THAT I DO--
AND TRUST THAT WHAT YOU THINK IS BEST FOR YOU ACTUALLY MIGHT BE.

I'M GOING TO BE A LOT BETTER NOW. ABOUT LETTING YOU BE WHO YOU ARE, ISAAC. AND, MIRIAM...
LEARNING MORE ABOUT WHO YOU ARE.

MOM, I'M SORRY WE DIDN'T TELL YOU. ABOUT EVERYTHING--
NO NEED TO APOLOGIZE. I UNDERSTAND.
FROM NOW ON, WE'LL START EMBRACING WHAT MAKES YOU... YOU.

SKETCHBOOK
SWAMPS + SORCERY

NOW, MAYBE YOU CAN SHOW ME A LITTLE ABOUT HOW THIS GAME IS PLAYED.
ARE THERE GAME PIECES? TOKENS?

...SOMETIMES THERE ARE.
BUT REALLY, ALL YOU NEED TO PLAY SWAMPS & SORCERY IS PENCILS, PAPER, A FEW BOOKS, AND SOMEONE WHO WANTS TO BRING EVERYONE ON AN ADVENTURE...

YOU CAN CHOOSE THREE ABILITIES.
OK...LET'S SEE...
GOT MINE ALREADY! DEADLIFTING, WALL CLIMBING, AND ACROBATICS.
I SENSE A THEME!

I THINK I'M ACTUALLY DONE! MAYBE I CAN START TODAY.
HAVE FUN...

H-HEY.

SORRY! WE'VE NEVER HAD THIS MANY PEOPLE OVER...
NEXT TIME WE'LL DO BETTER.

I ACTUALLY LIKE YOUR HOUSE. IT'S COZY.
REALLY?
REALLY.

I'M...SO GLAD YOU'RE HERE, MICAH. THAT WE'RE ALL HERE...BUT THAT YOU'RE HERE.

ME TOO...

JUST A BUNCH OF WEIRDOS, PLAYING THEIR WEIRD GAME.

SILENCE!
IT IS IN MY CHARGE TODAY TO CONTINUE TO GM THE TOWER OF GREENMOON, THROUGH WHICH SOME OF YOU HAVE JOURNEYED LONG, AND OTHERS ARE NEW.

SO NOW THAT WE'VE GATHERED, IT'S TIME TO QUIET YOUR CHATTER AND RETURN TO THE GILDED HALLS OF THE TOWER, WHERE A PERILOUS ASCENSION AWAITS.

YOU'RE SURE IT'S OK IF WE JUST JOIN IN?
IS IT *OK?* NAY, ADVENTURER. IT IS REQUIRED!
THE TOWER OF GREENMOON OPENS ITS WONDROUS GATES TO ALL, WITH ITS MYSTERIES AND ILLUSIONS.

HEY, MAN, AS LONG AS BOBBERT GETS TO KEEP ROCKING!
GRUNTUS!

♫ NOW WE'RE RETURNING TO THE TOWER OF GREENMOON!
IT'S TIME TO FIGHT MONSTERS AND EXPLORE ALL THESE WEIRD ♫ ♪ ROOMS!

ARE YOU READY, SER BRIDGER?
I AM. WHAT ABOUT YOU, MASTER VOLIN?
I STAND READY.

YOU'VE SEEN MUCH THROUGHOUT YOUR TRAVELS--
FROM CURSED FORESTS THAT EBB YOUR HOPES, TO CAVERNS THAT ROB OF YOU OF YOUR MOST PRECIOUS MEMORIES...
...BUT NOTHING COULD HAVE PREPARED YOU FOR WHAT YOU SEE BEFORE YOU NOW...
THIS TOWER YOU'VE ARRIVED IN, FROM THE INSIDE, BARELY SEEMS LIKE A TOWER AT ALL. BUT LIKE A BRAND-NEW EXPANSE OF LAND, WITH A BRIGHT-BLUE HORIZON.

THE ONLY DIFFERENCE IS THE COLOR OF THE SUN. GREEN. BRIGHT GREEN. SO GREEN THAT YOU LOOK DOWN AT YOUR MAGIC RINGS TO SEE IF THEY MATCH THE COLOR.
"YOU REALIZE THAT IN FACT, THEY DO. YOU THEN LOOK AROUND YOU AT YOUR FRIENDS, OLD AND NEW, CONSIDERING BOTH THE ADVENTURES YOU'VE BEEN THROUGH AND THE ONES TO COME. FOR A MOMENT, YOU RECALL THE TOILS OF THE PAST, BUT THEN, THE LIGHT OF THE FUTURE SHINES BRIGHT, AND YOU KNOW YOUR CAMARADERIE WILL OUTLAST THE DARKNESS.
"FOR ALTHOUGH THE SMALL, SIMPLE WORLD MAY TRY AND SHRINK YOU IN ITS SIGHTS, IN EACH OTHER YOU SEE EXACTLY HOW UNIQUE EACH AND EVERY ONE OF YOU ARE."

A WARNING TO INTERLOPERS, MALEFACTORS, AND LICKSPITTLES OF ALL PERSONAGES AND SPECIES...HEREIN LIE THE WORDS OF QUEST MAGISTRATE CARMEN LINDO, FIRST MAGUS OF GREENMOON AND PURVEYOR OF FATES. READING THE ENTRIES WITHIN WILL RESULT IN YOUR COMPLETE PHYSICAL DESTRUCTION, AND YOUR SOUL WILL BE KEPT FOR BARTER IN THE MARKETS OF RAKUL.

the quest for Greenmoon

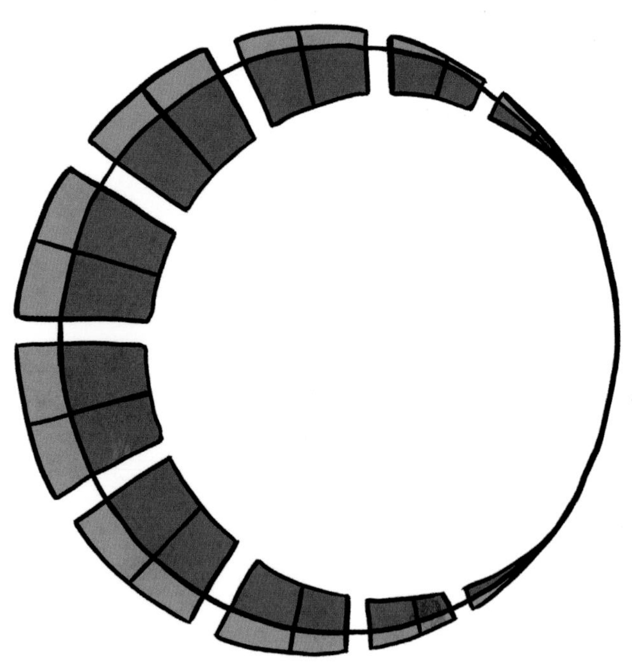

CORVIDA'S NOTCH

CAMPAIGN TITLE: THE PORKY SWALLOW
TERRAIN: FOREST, TAVERN
TOTAL GP: VARIABLE
ENEMY XP: 1800
SETUP: EACH PC HAS ARRIVED SEPARATELY AT THE PORKY SWALLOW, SEEKING FOOD AND SHELTER AFTER EXHAUSTIVE JOURNEYS THAT HAVE LED THEM TO CORVIDA'S NOTCH.

Opening dialogue (GM to ensure she is wearing her conjurer's cloak and is prepared to speak in ominous baritone): "It's been an unusually cold month, particularly as Corvida's Notch is concerned. Travelers rarely require more than light silks in spring when traveling through this valley, but everyone you've crossed thus far has complained of an unnatural, winter-like chill. Each of you adventurers ended up in Corvida's Notch for different reasons, but what all you have in common is that you're far from home, and you've come to rest at an inn called the Porky Swallow."

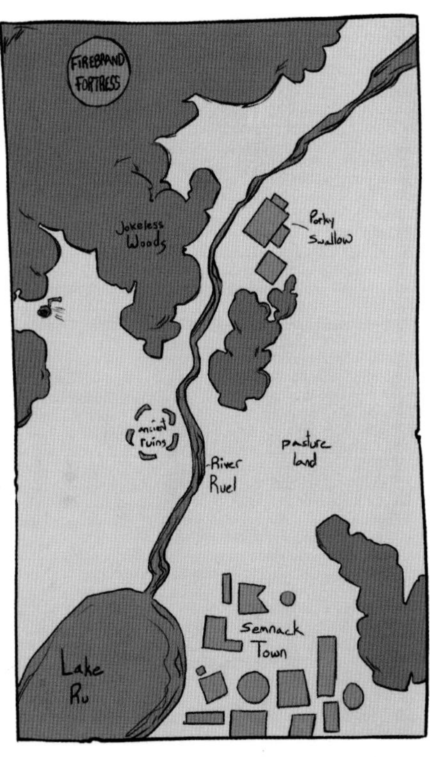

The Porky Swallow: Set to the side of a path well-trodden by horse hooves and wagon wheels stands a welcoming inn surrounded by patches of peat moss and thick-leafed trees. The sign for the Porky Swallow swings creakily in the wind, exhibiting a humble swallow with a pig's snout. The inn's facade has a faint trace of mist that seems to stick to its bottom, near the foundations, just a trace of it. Though it's still light out, the approaching evening has a large lantern lit, near the bar sign on a post. The insides of the tavern itself (see exhibit 1A for details)

is at three-fourth's capacity. Humans, gnomes, and Kora'lgal-resembling humanoid rapscallions sit at tables, drinking and eating and telling inane tales. The barkeep is an old, seemingly elvish woman with a haggard disposition and a head wrap covering her silver hair. To her right, floating over her shoulder, is her flying octopus familiar. Also of note—the tavern's basement contains an enchanted mirror containing Lister's original form. More shall be explained as we sally forth.

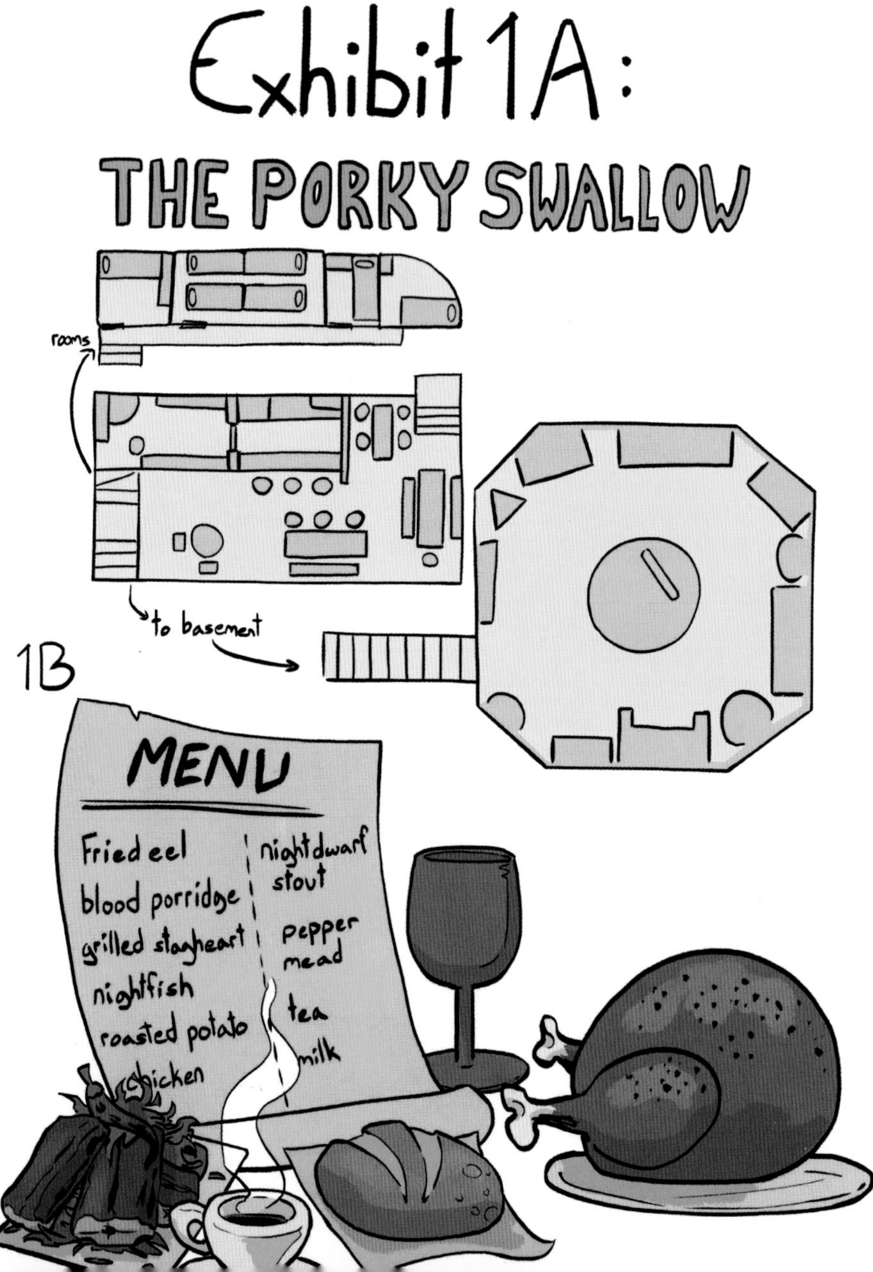

LISTER

An old woman with walnut skin and eyes as silver as her hair, she stands behind the counter with her floating octopus familiar, Mog. When the PCs ask for food, she refers them to a menu (see exhibit 1B for details). Lister is hiding a secret from the characters, in that she's been expecting them due to the spectacular Prophecy of Greenmoon, of which I have singularly compiled full documentation in *Archives of the Vanishing Tower, Volumes One through Three*!

Exhibit 2: The Order of The Steel Sun

The PCs will soon be compelled to intervene on Lister's behalf when threatened by Lyla von Flood, chief inquisitor of the Order of the Steel Sun, an empire-sanctioned group of power-mad crusaders attempting to rid the land of perceived evil...or rather anything that runs contrary to the Temple of Jadum.

THE PLAYER CHARACTERS

SER BRIDGER LIGHTBORN, HUMAN PALADIN

PRONOUNS: THEY/THEM

ALIGNMENT: LAWFUL GOOD

BACKGROUND: A PALADIN OF CRUCAS, SERVANT TO JUSTICE AND DEFENDER OF THE WEAK

CATCHPHRASE: "I WILL DO WHAT MUST BE DONE."

ARMOR CLASS: 13
HIT POINTS: 9 (1D8 +1)
SPEED: 40 FT.
STR: 13
DEX: 10
CON: 10
INT: 13
WIS: 16
CHA: 14

BOBBERT THE BRITTLE, ORC BARD

ARMOR CLASS: 12
HIT POINTS: 7 (1D6 +1)
SPEED: 30 FT.
STR: 11
DEX: 13
CON: 10
INT: 13
WIS: 12
CHA: 17

PRONOUNS: HE/HIM

ALIGNMENT: CHAOTIC GOOD

BACKGROUND: MOSTLY UNEMPLOYED HEAVY-METAL LUTIST

CATCHPHRASE: "ROCK TILL YOU **DROP**...SOME MAGICAL ITEMS."

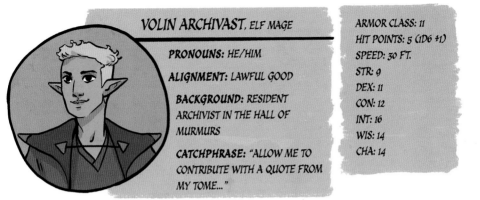

VOLIN ARCHIVAST, ELF MAGE

PRONOUNS: HE/HIM

ALIGNMENT: LAWFUL GOOD

BACKGROUND: RESIDENT ARCHIVIST IN THE HALL OF MURMURS

CATCHPHRASE: "ALLOW ME TO CONTRIBUTE WITH A QUOTE FROM MY TOME..."

ARMOR CLASS: 11
HIT POINTS: 5 (1D6 +1)
SPEED: 30 FT.
STR: 9
DEX: 11
CON: 12
INT: 16
WIS: 14
CHA: 14

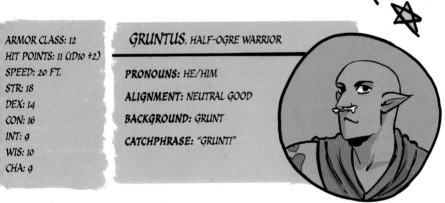

GRUNTUS, HALF-OGRE WARRIOR

PRONOUNS: HE/HIM

ALIGNMENT: NEUTRAL GOOD

BACKGROUND: GRUNT

CATCHPHRASE: "GRUNT!"

ARMOR CLASS: 12
HIT POINTS: 11 (1D10 +2)
SPEED: 20 FT.
STR: 18
DEX: 14
CON: 16
INT: 9
WIS: 10
CHA: 9

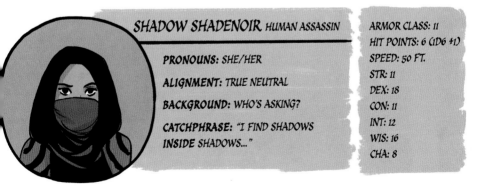

SHADOW SHADENOIR HUMAN ASSASSIN

PRONOUNS: SHE/HER

ALIGNMENT: TRUE NEUTRAL

BACKGROUND: WHO'S ASKING?

CATCHPHRASE: "I FIND SHADOWS INSIDE SHADOWS..."

ARMOR CLASS: 11
HIT POINTS: 6 (1D6 +1)
SPEED: 50 FT.
STR: 11
DEX: 18
CON: 11
INT: 12
WIS: 16
CHA: 8

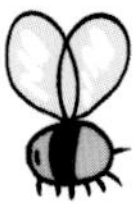

Author's Note

The word *neurodivergent* has become common in its usage, and I'm sure many of you have heard it before, possibly referring to a friend, family member, or even yourself. That's what I am, anyhow: neurodivergent. I have a brain that works a little differently from what others consider the norm.

Personally, I was diagnosed with obsessive-compulsive disorder when I was fourteen, though my father, who also has OCD, said he saw me exhibiting symptoms as young as six. OCD, like many mental-health issues, is often misunderstood. How many times have you heard someone say, "I am *so* OCD!" when chuckling about how attentive they are to cleanliness or scheduling? For those of us who have the disorder, thinking of it as something that keeps you organized doesn't compute, since we often can be disorganized and, without treatment, stand by helplessly as our lives spin out into neglect.

By definition, OCD is a disorder in which intrusive, unwanted thoughts and preoccupations, called *obsessions*, consume an affected person's daily life, resulting in *compulsions* to expel the obsessions. These compulsions manifest physically in terms of rituals and/or physical tics. Unwanted thoughts can focus on contamination, harm, and/or psychosomatic sensations. Regardless of what kind of thoughts OCD produces (which can evolve over time), the result is usually that the person with the disorder often ends up looking at themselves as if they're contaminated/deformed, unlikable, or unlovable. Recognizing OCD comes along with an official diagnosis from a psychiatrist or psychotherapist.

Throughout my life, my neurodivergence sometimes led me to thinking I wasn't deserving of love in some way or another and couldn't live a "normal" existence. But then, over time, a shift occurred. Not just through therapy (though that was and remains very important), but also through learning that my definitions of "weird" and "normal" were unimaginative. The discovery of books, art, and TTRPGs (tabletop roleplaying games) showed me a universe where the definition of "normal" could shift. With TTRPGs especially, literal new worlds opened up, where my character could be anyone and make choices that I wouldn't have access to in everyday life. Playing them improved my mental health and allowed me room to express myself. And I know I'm not alone. Many people with mental differences have used TTRPGs as a way to safely explore themselves to positive results. And the benefits aren't just limited specifically to mental-health disorders or being differently abled, but to those who would like to explore and expand upon identity in various ways, including race and gender roles.

If we have the room to rethink what "weird" is, the definition of "normal" changes. Because what is normal, anyway? This word we use to talk about what's acceptable and what's not follows us around every day, asking if we're living up to ideas laid out by people who might mean well but assume too much. Though there's nothing wrong with trying to set standards, the truth is that many of us simply operate differently from others through no fault of our own. If you're one of those people, then this story is for you. Rye and I have created *Buzzing* for the weird kids. The kinds of people who truly change the world just by being who they are. Hopefully this book will help you recognize your own beautiful weirdness and give you the power to control and then embrace it.

Acknowledgments

I'd like to thank my partner, Janelle, for their support, encouragement, and love for this book. My studiomates—David, Jeremy, Jorge, Morgan, and Sarah—for vent sessions and telling me the art looked good, even on days when I wasn't so convinced.

A huge thank-you to Kayton Uvick for being the best flatter in the entire history of comics. And to Dara Hyde, agent extraordinaire, whose thoughtfulness and care for this book safeguarded it during the whole journey. To Aria Balraj, whose instincts for emotional depth and big-nerd silliness shaped *Buzzing* into its best self. And to Andrea Colvin for seeing a *Buzzing*-shaped hole in the universe.

And a massive thank-you to my cats, Habibi and Maya, for not knocking any coffee onto my computer as I drew, and for keeping the amount of cat hair stuck to my tablet to a minimum. A similar thank-you to Hector for being the wiggliest and best studio pup-slash-HR-substitute an artist could have.

—Rye Hickman

A book like *Buzzing* doesn't happen without a village of inspirators. First off, to Rye, big-minded, big-hearted, big-talented copilot and the coolest of beans. I'd like to thank editor Andrea Colvin for being *Buzzing*'s great champion. All hats are off to super-agent Dara Hyde, best in the biz, watcher on the wall, etcetera and forthwith. To Aria Balraj for guiding *Buzzing* through its twistiest turns and bringing out its deepest potential. To my friends, family, and colleagues, who tolerated my endless excitement about this project over the last few years. To Inigo Montoya, who substituted my keyboard wrist pad, and to Leeloo, who coolly observed his boldness. And lastly, to books, writing, and TTRPGs, all of which helped me quiet my own thought bees and learn to live alongside them.

—Sam Sattin

About the Author & Illustrator

Samuel Sattin is an author and coffee addict. He is the adapter of Cartoon Saloon's Academy Award–nominated Irish Folklore trilogy to the graphic novel format, and is writing a reimagining of the Osamu Tezuka character Unico for a new manga series. His past work includes *Bezkamp* and *The Silent End*. He graduated with an MFA in comics from California College of the Arts and a creative writing MFA from Mills College, and lives in Oakland, California. He invites you to visit him at samuelsattin.com, on his Instagram @samuelsattin, and on Twitter @SamuelSattin.

Rye Hickman is a visual storyteller and a graduate of the Savannah College of Art and Design's sequential art program. Their past work includes *Lonely Receiver*, *TEST*, *Moth & Whisper*, and more. They get really excited about dystopian fiction, good coffee, and drawing hands. They invite you to visit them at ryehickman.com, on their Instagram @ryehickmandraws, and on Twitter @ryehickman.